KATHI S. BARTON

This is a work of fiction. Names, characters, places, and incidents are products of the author's imagination or are used fictitiously and are not to be construed as real. Any resemblance to actual events, locations, organizations, or person, living or dead, is entirely coincidental.

WCP

World Castle Publishing, LLC
Pensacola, Florida

ISBN: 9781938961113
First Edition World Castle Publishing, LLC, July 15, 2012
http://www.worldcastlepublishing.com

Cover: Karen Fuller
Photos: Shutterstock.com
Editor: Brieanna Robertson

Chapter One

"So, let me get this straight. I can borrow five hundred dollars to use toward a car that costs a grand as long as I have collateral. I can use the six hundred dollars that I currently have in the bank as that, but I can't touch it until the loan is paid back. And I can't borrow a grand because I don't have enough collateral. You know, that doesn't really make any sense. If I could leave my money in the bank, I would. But you see, I need to have a car. Without a car, I can't work; without work, the six hundred is going to be gone in no time anyway." Tess stared at the woman behind the desk and waited—for what? She wasn't sure, maybe divine intervention or a bundle of money to fall into her lap. But she really did not think either was going to happen.

She had the money, she supposed, enough money to buy several cars if she wanted. But she had never touched the money from her first job and she had no intention of doing so now. As far as she was concerned, it was blood money. She was getting along just fine with her bartending money and she would continue, thank you very much.

A tingle at the back of her neck had her turn her head slightly. She pretended to rub her chin on her shoulder as she looked around the bank. Nothing seemed out of place, but something was not quite right. Opening herself up, she lightly touched each person in the bank.

There were ten people milling about the counters on the bank side, three of them were shape-shifters, werewolves. The two tellers behind the glass screen were both human and the one at the desk back there was fae. The other four were humans as well.

Tess could see that of the eight people in line, two were unknown to her, meaning they could be lesser witches or some other creatures, but not human. Of the others there was one fairy, another fae, and a shape-shifter, this one a panther. The woman Tess was sitting with and the other bank assistant were both wolves.

Turning back to the assistant, Tess decided that Tansy Wolff was not going to change her mind about the money and started to rise. When she did, the tingle started again. This time Tess moved deeper and, closing her eyes, found what she was looking for. Opening her eyes, she looked at her "personal banker."

"Call the cops. There is a robbery going to happen right now. The two men standing by your guard over in the front are carrying weapons that are loaded with silver. They are expecting six more any moment now."

Tess was sure that Tansy was going to balk or try something incredibly stupid like demand proof, but she simply nodded and picked up her phone. As she laid it back in the cradle she was shaking her head.

"Phone is dead. I can't make any calls. But I can reach my…boss and tell him, but it may take a while for him to get here."

"Boss? I take it you don't mean the one here. Your alpha, you mean? We don't have much of a choice unless you know some other way to contact someone." When she didn't answer, Tess stood up and stuck out her hand. "Take my hand and it will open a pathway for us. It won't hurt you, but I need to have a set of eyes where you will be taken."

"What about you? Where will you be taken?" Tansy took her hand and Tess felt the immediate connection.

"I won't." And she shimmered from the room. "The other men have just pulled up outside. Keep the others that are with you from panicking. And call to me if you have any problems."

The door burst open and five men entered the bank and opened fire. Their automatic weapons tore large holes in the ceiling and walls and it rained down on the customers. Every person in the place dropped to the floor and put their hands over their heads. Tellers behind the glass hit the alarm buttons, but to no avail. The power had been cut to those as well as all the security cameras.

"I want everyone to stay where you are. If you think to be a hero, you'll be a dead one. I have no problem shooting every last one of you to get what I want," the man who came in after the guns went off stated as he sauntered into the room.

Brian Manchester did not wear a mask, nor did he carry a gun. He felt that there was no reason for either. The muscle he had with him would do as he said, or he would kill them as well. Tess knew this; she had seen it in his mind. He was ruthless, vicious, and he had done this several times before, killing everyone in the other banks just as he had planned to do here. Well, she thought, not on her watch.

Brian made his way to the manager's office and only took one man that he brought with him. Two were left by the door, two more started empting the cash drawers behind the glass, and the last two started gathering the employees and customers together to take them to the back offices. Tansy was a part of this group, hidden from them but able to keep up with the robbers too.

Tess kept herself shadowed in the dark corners as she walked up behind the first two men who were just finishing the cash drawers. One of them was human, the other a shifter. Killing the human would be quicker, but the shifter would be stronger and would definitely fight back. Taking a long, silver blade from her boot, she appeared between them and struck. She slit the wolf's throat open and then stabbed the human in the heart, killing him instantly. Catching both men as they fell, she laid them as quietly as she could on the floor. Taking out a silver chain, she laid it across the open wound of the wolf and stepped over him. With the silver there he would not be able to shift to heal, and before his friends found him later and removed the silver he would have bled out.

Fading out again, she moved toward the vault where she knew there were three other men. The bank manager was with Brian and a human robber. Before she moved forward she paused to listen to them.

"This will make us even, Mr. Manchester, right? The fifty million I owe you will be wiped off the books, right?" Nervousness colored the manager's voice, making it squeaky and high.

Fifty million was a lot to owe to just one person and she wondered what the bank manager was into so deep. She then realized that it didn't matter how he got to this point. It was how he was getting himself out that put these people into danger.

"Of course it will, Tommy. Isn't that what we agreed on? You make sure the vault is open for me and I make sure you don't owe me another penny. You don't sound very trusting right now." Brian sounded bored and condescending. Tess did not believe for a moment that he was going to let Tommy's debt be paid.

"No! No, that's not it. I just…you know with the audit coming on and all, I don't want to lose my job over that missing money is all. I have to keep up appearances and all, you know." His grin looked sad and scared even to Tess, but she didn't waste much sympathy on him.

"Of course. Of course. This is going to work out just fine, just fine indeed."

Tess watched as Tommy finished opening the vault. When the door swung open Brian pulled a gun from the man next to him and shot Tommy in the head. Just that quick, Tommy's debt was paid and he was dead.

She watched as the two robbers stepped over Tommy's body and went into the vault. It was then that Tansy spoke to Tess.

"Hello, Miss Knight, I have a problem. Can you come here? Like right fucking now?"

Leaving the men inside, Tess moved to where Tansy was, the urgency in her voice making Tess move quickly.

One of the men had decided to have a little fun with one of the customers. Tansy was trying to fight him, but she was limited in her abilities because of the humans in the room. She could not shift and she could not use her superior strength to subdue without causing problems for her and the pack in which she belonged to. Tess, however, had no such problems.

Stepping out of the room to become solid, she moved back in and grabbed the man who was trying to rape one of the women and tossed him out into the hall; the other man did not move. He either didn't care or, more than likely, he thought that his partner would kill her. Now, without prying eyes, Tess pulled out her knife and began fighting the man.

He was strong, and as a wolf he would be, but he was also quick and high on something. He was on his feet again before she could move and had slammed her against the wall in seconds. Stabbing him in his shoulder was all she could manage with the quickness of the fight, and the small wound only seemed to make him madder. He wrapped his hand around her throat and, as he began to squeeze, he ripped at her clothes. When he had exposed her bra he grabbed at her breast and twisted. Pain shot through her and she kicked out, knocking him away briefly. When he came at her this time she was more prepared and caught him in the nose with her fist, breaking it and her hand.

She had meant to shove the little bones into his brain, killing him, but he was taller than her and her aim was a little off because of the pain in her breast. But it did knock him back again. This time, while he was stunned, she kicked him hard in the balls. She managed to kick him again and again before he fell to the floor holding himself. When he bent his head over she pulled her belt free of the loops and wrapped it around his massive neck. The silver studs and the leather tightened into his skin as he tried to struggle out of the hold. When he began to black out, Tess pulled out her knife again and rammed it into his heart from behind. He dropped like the dead weight he was. She knew she would have to leave the blade there and mourned the loss of one of her favorite knives.

Hearing a noise behind her, she turned and nearly hit the woman who had come up behind her. Tansy had the good sense to back up and blush.

"My alpha is here. He and the pack are outside. He wants to know how many are left. He also said to tell you to sit tight that he will be inside soon. He thinks he needs to be the big brother and save my ass and the others." Tansy's grin told Tess that she either was used to his intervention or aggravated by it—probably both.

Tess snorted, leaned against the wall, and tried to repair her shirt. Her boob hurt and she thought she had a broken rib or two. Looking down at her hand, she knew it was probably sprained and not broken like she had thought, but was otherwise all right.

"Tell him that there were eight to begin with, now there are only five. Oh, and the manager, Tommy somebody, was in on the entire thing. He was letting the leader into the vault when he was murdered. He owed some money to the robbers. Tommy is dead now because they no longer had any use for him," Tess told her.

"He was an idiot. Not that I'd wish him dead. But you play with these guys, you have to accept a shorter life expectancy."

"Well, he got it. But I would keep his death to yourself with the cops. They'll know you weren't there when he was killed and wonder how you know anything about it."

Tansy nodded in understanding. "What about you sitting tight? What would you like for me to tell him about that?"

Tess looked at Tansy and grinned. "Tell him to fuck off. Please."

Tess made sure that the others were all right; the other robber had left them alone by leaving the area. Good, Tess thought. As she went back into the main part of the bank, Tess saw the two men posted at the front door. They were both well armed and were staying back far enough from the windows so as not to become a target from the police. The police must have arrived sometime while Tess was in the back with Tansy. Tess decided to let the two of them go for the moment.

There were no hostages with them and they were keeping the police out of her way for the moment. She headed back to the vault.

Brian and the other man were loading bank bags with the money. They had also opened a few of the safety deposit boxes along the walls and had emptied the contents as well. Tommy lay in his own blood and since Tess could not help him, she ignored him.

Waiting for the right moment, she watched the two of them. They seemed to know just which boxes to open. This made some sense, if she thought about it. With Tommy's help they would know which ones held nothing of value. They would only need to open the ones that had something of worth in them. But that did not seem to be the case. The other man was touching each box and marking it. From where she stood Tess could not see how he was doing it, so she moved closer to him. She felt when he knew she was there the second before he turned.

He was clairvoyant. Tess grabbed his arm and jerked it up and behind him. He was still human, but his brainwaves where incredible. It mattered little to her at the moment and she wrapped her hand over his brain and pushed herself into him mentally, absorbing all that he knew. His scream echoed throughout the little room.

Even though Brian could not see her, nor feel where she was, he did know that something was happening to his partner. So when Brian pulled the gun out again and started firing she simply turned and let him shoot his man. The bullets ripped into the clairvoyant's heart, killing him instantly.

Tess dropped her shield and grabbed the gun as it went off again. Pain moved through her in an instant, but she could not let him get the upper hand or she would be dead. Brian had been practicing the dark arts and his magic was strong, but not as strong as Tess.

Opening her palm and her physical form to Brian, she pressed her hand to his face and pushed all that she had taken from the other man into Brian—the man's memories, his thoughts, but mostly his abilities. Power surged into him and the room swelled with it.

She watched as he grinned, thinking she had boosted him with her touch. She had really, but there was no reason to share with him that it was only a temporary feeling. Brian had neither the ability to use the mind ability, nor the knowledge to use it.

When he reached out to touch her, Tess backed up. She saw the pain register on his face, just a small twitch of it at first. Then the vein in his forehead began to expand and pulse. He dropped the gun and pressed his hands to his head and groaned.

"It'll only get worse from here. Next your eyes will start to bleed, then your nose. As your ears begin to fill with blood you'll become deaf from the pressure. But that will be all right. When you start screaming, you won't be able to hear yourself."

"Hurts! My God, it hurts. What have you done?" Brian moaned.

"I overloaded your brain. It won't kill you, at least not very fast, but you'll wish it would. You won't be able to see soon. The vessels in your eyes will swell and then your eyes will explode. I've seen a person after that happens; the sockets are just empty holes in their heads. Kind of an ugly sight—no pun intended. Anyway, that won't be so bad. After a few days you're going to start to hallucinate about feeling things on your body. That will drive you to the point of no return, but by then you'll be locked up and there won't be any way for them to help you. This could go on for years."

Tess watched as he absorbed her tale. The only part that was true was that she had overloaded his brain for a few seconds. The rest she had implanted in his brain to make him think he was in pain. She turned to walk away to leave the man to his misery. She needed to take care of the front door now that the others were taken care of. A gunshot sounded behind her as she walked into the main lobby.

"Tansy, it's Tess Knight. I'm going to open the front doors now. The two up here are all that's left of the would-be robbers. Once the police come in they'll want to know about Tommy. You don't need to tell them anything. There is going to be an audit soon, that'll tell them what they need."

"Yes, I knew about that. You're sure he was involved? No, don't answer that, I know you are. What should I tell my alpha? He'll want to talk to you, I'm sure."

Tess looked down at the wound in her belly and cringed. It was bad, and there would be very little anyone could do about it at this point. She had lost too much blood. Pressing her hand back over it, she nearly passed out from the pain. Yes, she thought, not much longer now.

"Tell him . . . tell him that I said thank you and that I couldn't have done it without you. You saved that woman back there, and because of your help no one that didn't deserve it was killed. Thanks."

"Tess, if you come back in after this is over I'll make sure you get the money you need to buy that car. You saved us all."

"I'll do that. I have to get rid of these two. It won't be much longer now."

Tess closed off the connection and pulled the shadows around her. There was not much time to mess with these two. She was getting weaker by the moment. Tess moved between them and she pulled the first man's hand with the gun in it toward the other man and fired, shooting him three times in the chest point blank. The man who held the gun reached for Tess with his other hand just as she put his gun under his chin and fired.

She dropped to the floor with them. Her body was spent. As she crawled away from the dead men she heard the first cop enter from the back; he and his men came in hard, hot, and armed. Grinning, she thought of the mess he was going to find back there and sobered.

Poor stupid, misguided Tommy had been killed because he had been greedy. It was simply bad choices that Brian had been the one who had "rescued" him.

The front door exploded open as she rounded the corner into the little office she had spotted earlier. That was as far as she could go and collapsed. Her last thought was she should have put her money in the bank across town.

Chapter Two

"There are nine dead men and one critically injured woman who I'm not entirely sure is human. Eight of the men are the would-be robbers; the ninth is the bank manager, Thomas Bentley. The woman, Tess Knight, was a customer, the woman Tansy told us about. Ms. Knight will be lucky if she makes it out of the bank alive. She was shot in the lower abdomen and has lost a lot of blood, too much according to the EMT."

Bradley nodded at his brother David. Tansy had told him that the woman had saved their lives and had it not been for her one of the women, one of his pack members, would have been raped as well. He hoped Aaron made it in time to save Tess. His blood was the strongest Bradley knew of.

Aaron MacManus was his friend and a Master Vampire. With his age and magical powers Aaron could stand the sun more than a normal vamp could.

"I don't believe she is either, human I mean. Tansy said that she could move in shadows like a vamp. David, make sure she is transported to the clinic and that just pack is with her. We are going to try and hold her here for Aaron, but it's still too early for him to rise. Sara is driving here, but it will take too long for her to get here too. Christ, this is a cluster fuck. Do we know what happened in there?"

"No. Tansy said that Tess told her before it happened what was going down. She said that Tess knew that six men were going to join the two that were already here. She also told Tansy to not say anything about Tommy being in on it to the police, that the audit next week would be telling enough. You don't think this Tess may have been in on it from the beginning, do you?"

"No, but I don't want to take any chances. Restrain her, but nothing else. We don't want anyone else hurt because we didn't know. What else? What aren't you telling me?"

Bradley may have been David's brother, but David was also a cop and a damn good one. He would have more information than he might be able to legally give Bradley, but as David's alpha he would give him information he would not be able to share with any of the men and women he worked with.

"She has a mark, a tat on her arm. It's a crest of some sort; I think it's called a sigil. I've never seen it before. Can you take a look when she comes out? I've not made a big deal of it; most of the men think it's just at tattoo. It has a set of crossed daggers on it, but doesn't really look like Sara's."

A mark could mean a lot or nothing at all, Bradley knew. But lately he knew that it would mean a hell of a lot, especially if there was magic involved. Deep down, he knew that something was about to hit the fan. Again. He smiled. There was never a dull moment in their little part of Ohio.

He started making a mental note of things he would need to do. First, he would need to contact the queen. Mel would need to be notified about the mark as soon as possible. She was the Queen of Magic and the overseer of all magic used. Sara, Aaron's mate and the cousin to the queen, had a mark, or sigil, that marked her as a Brianal. It was the Tree of Seasons, but with one difference. Sara's had a pair of crossed claymores under it, marking her as a member of the Brianal Guard as well. Pete, another woman in Aaron's Kiss, had a mark too, but hers was a mark of her heritage as a Brianal and a wood nymph. He could only wonder what magic this woman would bring to the Kiss.

Rubbing his hand over his face Bradley knew it was a moot point if the girl did not live. And he looked at his watch again. Damn it, still at least another twenty minutes before anyone would be here to save her.

Bradley felt the vampire before he saw him. He had been around enough of them lately to know that the pinched feeling he got in the back of his neck signaled one was near, and from the amount of pain he knew the vamp was a strong one. He looked around and spotted him leaning against one of the cruisers. Reaching out to David, he had him go toward the man too.

When they were close enough, the man stood and pulled his hands out of his pockets. He raised his hand slightly to show that he had no weapon, but not high enough to draw attention to them.

"Alpha. Captain. Nice night, wouldn't you say? I'm going to reach into my pocket and pull out my badge and ID, all right?"

As the man reached in, Bradley did the same and handed it to him. David had his badge out already, but did take his hand off his gun and relax. The vamp handed his things to David. When he was finished David handed them to Bradley.

"Nathaniel Tremont. It says you're with the FBI; want to tell me what you are doing on my streets at my crime scene, Agent Tremont?" David asked him as he looked around the scene. He wondered if David was looking for other vampires.

"Nothing. I saw the lights and came to see if I could be of any help. But it looks like you guys have it under control. I would like to ask if one of the men was Brian Manchester. He's wanted in several bank robberies in eight states. I've been hunting him for several weeks now."

"Yeah, but he's dead. Looks like a self inflicted gunshot to the left temple. You can be of help, if you will. The woman who helped us out, actually did our work for us, is gravely injured and will more than likely not make it. Could you help us out?"

"No, I'm sorry, but I can't. I'm just a visitor passing through. It's dangerous to attach ourselves to people we don't know. I'm sure you understand." And Bradley stood as well, thinking he would stop him and try to talk him into please helping. Suddenly Nathaniel stiffened and looked over Bradley's shoulder.

"I would like for you to rethink that request. It could be very…beneficial to you to be smart right now. You don't strike me as a stupid man. I can usually tell when a vampire is being malicious, but you aren't. Are you? I mean, only a stupid vampire or a dead one would enter my territory without proper notifications." Bradley turned as Aaron spoke.

"No, sire, I'm not stupid or malicious. Nor do I wish to die. I was just passing through on a lead. I was nearly there when this happened."

"You've been here, what? Five—six days? Long enough to make a phone call or an appointment, I would think. You are aware of the rules, are you not? Do you know the penalty for trespassing into another Master realm without due process?"

Bradley looked at each man. Aaron seldom got upset, especially when it came to the laws governing his realm, but he was strict when the time warranted it. And it seemed Aaron felt this was one of those times.

The agent looked toward the bank and then back at Aaron. "She mean that much to you, sire? This woman, she means that much to you?"

"I don't know the woman. But according to my resources she saved the life of every being in that bank, including several members of this man's pack. Him I know and trust. And if he wants her saved, then I can do no less for him if that is what he wants. I'm sure you understand."

The sun was still pretty high in the sky yet and Bradley had not expected Aaron for at least another twenty minutes or so. It was then that Bradley realized the other vamp was out too. He turned back to him and stared, and before he could ask the agent, he answered for him.

"I'm old, and with that there comes certain…gifts." He looked at the bank again and sighed. "Do you know what you are asking me to do?"

"No. But I have a pretty good idea. You didn't just happened upon this scene any more than I did. Do you help her, or do I have to come up with a suitable punishment? The choice is up to you, Nathaniel."

Bradley heard the challenge in Aaron's tone and wondered about it. But Nathaniel only nodded and David took the four of them to the ambulance where Tess was being loaded.

The three wolves Bradley had sent to guard the woman moved to stop the agent and, when Bradley nodded to them, they stepped away. Tremont entered the ambulance and sat next to the bed as Aaron entered behind him. Bradley got into the front with the driver and they took off.

~~~

Nathaniel Tremont leaned down to the woman who was near death and inhaled. Christ, he thought, his mate. He leaned
~~~

back against the wall of the moving vehicle and looked at the master. The man was grinning like a loon.

"You know, I've often wondered if our mates smelled a way we would be familiar with or if they smelled like something that reflected their personalities. What does she smell like? You will save her for me, Nathaniel. What you do after that is up to the two of you."

"Saving her won't make her my mate; it will only make me want her more. You know that as well as I do. I have no need for one, or the time to train one."

"Train one? That's very funny. But it is true, I can't make you mate with her. But letting her die will get you killed, and I wouldn't be the only one you'd have to worry about either. Feed her or face me or the wolf up front. You may be older than me, but I can guarantee that I'm stronger. Healing her for us and for you could get you some major Brownie points with me. And I love giving out points for good behavior."

Nathaniel stared at him for a minute longer before opening his vein with his fang and pressing his wrist to Tess's soft mouth. She was very close to death; he could hear her heart beating softly within her chest. Reaching out with his other hand he tilted her head back and began to rub her throat, trying to get her to swallow. He wondered if he would be punished if she died anyway. Then he felt bad for such a horrible thought.

At first his blood trickled out of the corner of her mouth, then along her chin. He did not think she would take it. Then Aaron reached over him and closed off her nose. She would either swallow to breathe or suffocate. She swallowed.

Nathaniel continued to feed her until he could feel her heart responding to the power of his blood. The ambulance had pulled up in front of the clinic some five minutes before, but had not disturbed what was going on in the back, knowing that this was the only thing that would heal her and save her life.

When Nathaniel pulled his wrist away and sealed his open wounds she sighed heavily and turned her head toward him. She did not open her eyes, but smiled slightly. The doors opened and the two men standing there pulled her out on the gurney and rushed her inside.

Nathaniel turned to look at the vampire beside him again and sighed. He had heard about Aaron MacManus of course. Very few vampires had not. Aaron was known as a fair but consistent master, demanding very little of his people and giving back to them more than they had ever had with the previous master. He did not command often, but when he did his people would do his bidding willingly.

"You could have saved her yourself, you know. I'm not sure how you knew, but you did, didn't you? You knew she was my mate so why did you make me do it?"

"Yes. As did you before you got in the ambulance with her. If I gave her my blood she would always be a part of me. Later, if you decided to claim her, you could take exception to my part of her. Giving you the opportunity to save her leaves her safe and marked. How long have you been chasing her?"

"A couple of weeks now, I guess. She came across my path in Columbus at a job site where I had been working another murder. There was a slaughter of several beings. I don't believe she had anything to do with the deaths, but she did stay for some time. I'm not sure what she had been doing there, but I followed her scent here tonight. I was curious about her, nothing more. I didn't plan on approaching her at any point; I just wanted to see what she was."

"She isn't human, that's for sure. Her magic or power is strong and very familiar. She is somehow… I'll have someone see what they can find out about her. I want to thank you for showing up when you did. Let me know when you decide to leave, if you do leave at all. I would like to try and talk you into staying for a while. It would be nice to talk to someone around my age."

Nathaniel looked down at the hand the man was offering. He was not sure, but thought the man was mocking him somehow. Nathaniel shook Aaron's hand and turned to walk away. He had taken two steps when Aaron spoke again.

"My home is welcome to you while you're staying here, Nathaniel. There is plenty of room at the moment. The couple who were staying with us has recently built their own home and have only just moved out. You will be happy there. My children will not bother you overly much, and you can get your information about the bank robbery while you're there."

Somehow, Nathaniel knew it was not a request, but another command. He nearly refused the offer, but he was in the other man's territory and did not want to piss in anyone's oats.

"Sure, thanks. I'll just look around here for a little while and you let me know when you're ready to leave."

Aaron went into the clinic with Nathaniel not far behind.

Chapter Three

Tess woke but did not move. She had been in situations like this before. Where she had lost conciseness and woke in a strange place. Opening herself up she knew that one man, a wolf, was in the room with her and that she was in a medical facility of some sort, but not a hospital. There were not enough people for it to be a big one if she was.

There was a pair of handcuffs on her left wrist and another on her left ankle. Her belly was all but healed, just a few tender places here and there. She knew that someone, a vampire probably, had fed her his blood; she could almost feel his energy surging through her veins. There was also the metallic taste in her mouth. Not unpleasant like it normally was, but there nonetheless. The IV in her right hand was nothing more than glucose so she removed it as she turned toward the shifter.

"Where am I? And who do I have to kill to get out of here?" She was only slightly kidding, but still grinned at his expression.

"The Market Street Clinic and no one, I hope. As soon as you're released, you can go. Do you remember how you got here?"

"Yes. I killed six men and one of them tried to kill me back. Go figure. Do you know who fed me?"

"Fed you? Oh, you mean healed you. No, I don't. Some vamp, I guess. I'm day shift."

Tess sat up and the man rose as well. She looked down to where he had his hand on his weapon. He flushed and removed it and put his hands behind his back.

"Well, Officer Shift, I'm out of here. It's been real, but I have places to go." The cuffs fell off her and she moved to the side of the bed. He came to stand in front of her and she just raised a brow at him. "If you don't want me to hurt you, then I would suggest that you move."

"I don't think anyone expects you to want to leave just yet. They might have a few questions for you. You were cuffed to that bed. How did you…my alpha isn't going to be too happy if you leave without his permission."

"I'm sure he'll get over it," Tess said as she stood up.

The room tilted a little then righted itself. Holding onto the bed, she reached under the thing and took the big white bag that held her personal things to the bathroom.

Tess looked in the mirror over the sink. She was still surprised every time she saw this version of herself—the non-fae one. Her hair was basically the same only longer. And its color was no longer blue, but black—a shiny blue-black that was thick and heavy. It had some curl in it, a bounce she guessed, when it was short, which is how she wore it when she had been a guard for the Brianal Court. For now her hair was shoulder length and pulled in a ponytail at the back of her head most of the time. It had made it easier to keep out of her face.

It was her face that startled her the most; it was more human than fae. Her ears were rounded and smooth at the top now and, instead of the jewels that marked her, her lobes were now bare of anything. Her eyes were also different. Now they were more oval shaped and wider. She actually liked them. Before the change she had had eyes the color of polished pewter, now they were dulled silver. Pretty, but not hers. Her nose was small and had a slight tilt at the end, marking her for her aristocratic line. Her lower lip was full and looked pouty all the time. It was usually pink because she was forever nibbling on it. Her upper lip, while not as full as the lower, still looked kissable, she'd been told once by someone who thought she should let him kiss her before she killed him. Men. Long lashes swept across her high cheeks and her brows looked perfect even without having to have them groomed. But it was her height that made everyone notice her. She was six foot, three inches in her bare feet.

She would have loved to have time to shower, but knew that she was pushing it as it was. Instead, she pulled out her clothes and began to dress. She still had her panties on, but took them off. She hated to do it, but there was no way she was wearing them two days in a row—if it had only been two days. She pulled on her jeans, which were covered in blood, but no help for that she figured. Next was her shirt. She was just trying to decide if she could rinse out a little of her blood when there was a knock at the door. Damn it, she thought, time's up.

"I'll just be another second. I'm sure that there are other bathrooms on this floor if you need one in a hurry." She pulled the stained shirt over her head and opened the door to another wolf.

"I'd like to talk with you about a few things before you try to leave, Ms. Knight. And then there is a little matter of you killing nine men. You might need to explain that to someone at some point."

She glared at the man standing there. Alpha. She could feel his power, the man practically dripped with it, but she was not intimidated—well, not much anyway. She moved past him and pulled her boots out of the bag as she went.

"I did not kill nine men, one was killed by Manchester. And Manchester…he was alive when I left him. So if he's dead, then you figure it out." She sat down in the now vacant chair and started to put on her boots. She was suddenly exhausted and leaned back to look at the man.

She did not carry a purse, but it felt as if all her things were still in the pockets of her pants and in her boots. They had probably thought her too weak to get up and use any of them yet, if what the day shifter had told her was true. Well, she would certainly be able to change their minds on that if they tried to stop her.

"Tansy said a great deal about this savior of hers, how she saved everyone in that bank. And she said that you knew those men were coming before they entered the bank. Care to tell me how you knew?"

"No." Tess did not feel the need to fill the silences. She actually preferred the quiet over noise. She seldom, if ever, listened to the radio and did not own a television. Not that she could afford one, she thought, but still.

"Then would you like to tell me what you are? I don't think you're quite human, yet the wound in your stomach didn't look as if it was healing. You can pull shadows around yourself and move quickly like a vamp, yet you can be out in the daylight. You aren't wolf, or at least I don't think so, but I've been wrong before. Not often, but it's been known to happen. My mate thinks it happens more than I want to admit. Not that I'm correct, but that I'm more wrong than I think. But I don't believe her. Also, if you tell her, I'll deny it."

"Did you just crack a joke? Wow, who would have thought it—an alpha with a sense of humor? I'll have to write this in my diary. It'll say, 'alpha made a joke and is terrified of his mate.'" She stood up again and adjusted her boots tighter around her calves. As she strode toward the door, she felt rather than heard the alpha move.

She flipped around so quickly he did not have time to stop his forward momentum and she pinned him to the floor with a blade at his throat. His eyes widened when she pressed the knife a little deeper into his skin. She did not break skin, but she knew that he could smell the silver; the blade was pure.

"I didn't kill those men. They killed themselves when they walked into the bank armed and ready to kill anyone else that got in their way. Manchester killed Tommy and then Manchester killed himself. Did I have anything to do with that? Maybe. But as far as I'm concerned, they all got what they deserved. Now, I'm leaving and you're going to let me. There are people looking for me and I would just as soon they didn't find me. Whatever they want, it's too fucking late and I…never mind, they can't find me."

"I can help you, if you'd let me, Ms. Knight. I'm not without the means to make things happen for you. I owe you for my people's safety." She noticed that he had put his hands up as if he were surrendering to her.

"No. You're fine. The others? It's too little too late." She moved off of him, never taking the blade from his throat. When she stepped back he jumped to his feet, but made no effort to advance on her.

Backing her way to the door, she reached blindly behind her as she held the knife out toward the wolf. She reached for the handle and filled her hand with a man's cock. Turning quickly, she was pulled into the arms of the most beautiful man she had ever seen.

All she could see was his face, but that alone made her mouth water. His eyes were the deepest blue she had ever seen. And they seemed to see right into her soul. His hair was pulled back from his face, but she could see that it was blond with varying shades of browns, golds, and reds in it. His high forehead gave way to his dark brow, that was cocked at an angle that gave her the impression that they could and would say just as much as his words would. His lashes were long and dark as well, an envy of any woman in their thickness and length. Looking at his mouth made her think of long, wet, sensual kisses and, if he smiled, it would cause a woman's heart to skip several beats before it kicked into overdrive and made a woman pant with need to taste him. Tess had never seen a man with a square jaw, though she had heard the term. This man's was hard and covered in a shadow of dark whiskers. She wanted to lick it with every fiber of her being.

"Bradley. Hello there, Miss Knight. I'm Nathaniel Tremont. I'm an agent with the FBI and I'd like to ask you a few questions if you don't mind."

Tess turned and glared at the wolf, who was grinning like a he had just played a grand joke on her and had won. For now, she thought, but paybacks were a bitch. He had been a diversion, she realized then. Someone to keep her there until this man who held her had arrived. Well, she was having none of it.

"Am I under arrest? Have I done something to warrant you keeping here against my will, agent? Because if you are, then you can try and cuff me again if you think you can." She pulled away from him and felt the loss of his touch immediately. She then got angry with herself about feelings like that for a man who she did not know.

"No, ma'am. You're free to go. Like I said, I have a few questions I'd like to ask you, that's all. We can either do it here or down at the FBI office. Matters little to me, just whatever you're comfortable with," the agent said to her in an "I won't hurt a fly" voice.

She had a feeling her actual comfort mattered little in the large scheme of things. And he was right, she could do it here or downtown, but he would get his answers. She could see that in his eyes.

Tess knew that this man had fed her. For whatever reason, he had saved her life. She could feel the connection to him the moment she had touched him. She blushed slightly when she thought of her hand grabbing him like she had. His cock had been hard before she had touched it so she knew that she had not been the cause of how firm it had been under her fingers, but goodness, he was large and thick.

She looked up at him when he chuckled. She wondered if he could read her mind and then decided that she would test her theory. She tried to think of something really sexual and thought about her kneeling before him and unbuckling his belt, her fingers moving along the strip of leather, then unhooking the snap on his pants. Then she thought about the slow descent of his zipper and her hand reaching into his pants and freeing his cock from his briefs. Closing her eyes she thought about her tongue moving along the crest of him, the curved head hot with blood. Then she ran her tongue down the length of him, following the large vein from the top to the nest of curls at the base. Before she could go further in her thoughts, she opened her eyes when he had her pressed against the wall.

"You're playing with fire, little girl. Be careful you don't get scorched." He was panting and then she realized she was too. Her little experiment had gotten out of hand. But there was no reason for him to hold her like he was.

"Let me go."

"Not yet. You owe me." His mouth crushed over hers.

~~~

Nathaniel had never meant to claim her, much less kiss her. But her teasing him with her thoughts had gone too far. He
~~~

was already hard with wanting her and her mental video of them sent him over the top. He did not know how she did it, but she had fed him the same dream he had had about her just before sunrise. The only difference was they were in his chamber and not in a hospital room.

When she opened her mouth under his assault he groaned and slid his tongue along hers, tangling and mating with it. Her mouth was hot; her flavor was spicy and just what he thought she would taste like. He ground his cock hard against her soft folds and nearly snarled at her when she pulled her mouth from his. He moaned again when she nipped at his neck and chin, sending shivers of pleasure through his oversensitive body. Christ, he thought. He wanted her now.

"You two might want to wait until you're alone to finish this. I believe there are others coming in who might not enjoy watching the two of you fucking against the wall. But as I have said before, I could be wrong."

Nathaniel felt as if a bucket of cold water had been poured over his head. He jumped back from Tess quickly and then reached to steady her when she stumbled slightly. Her bared teeth and accompanying growl had him snapping his hand back quickly.

"I'm leaving and you will stay the fuck away from me." He felt the room fill with something, a tightening, then she was gone.

Nathaniel looked at the wolf. What the hell just happened? he wondered, and reached out to the wall to steady himself. Christ, but she was…power.

"You all right? I gotta tell you, vamp, I've never seen anything like it. You two glowed; I mean a huge fucking glow. I tried to look away, but it was like a train wreck. I just couldn't seem to pull my eyes off it. She is one nimble woman."

Nathaniel growled at the alpha and moved to hit him when he felt something coming toward the room.

The door opened and several beings walked into the room. Nathaniel would have to ask her to be sure of how Tess had disappeared so quickly, but one thing was certain, everyone was pissed that she was gone.

Aaron and four women entered and Nathaniel knew immediately why Aaron had told him that he was the stronger of the two of them. The powerbase that he kept company with was like nothing Nathaniel had ever experienced before. Walking in behind them, two men came in. The room seemed to expand under the weight of their combined magic. He knew that he was looking at pure magic, not the black he normally dealt with in his line of work.

"Where is she? I want to know where she's gone again. Damn it, Aaron, you said she would be here. Now where is she?" one of the women asked the master.

"If you mean Tess, then she left not ten seconds ago. She said that she was being hunted…well, she said that people where looking for her and she didn't want them to find her. Then they kissed and she left."

Nathaniel glared at the wolf and decided if he ever had the opportunity, he was going to drain the bastard. He did not seem to have a discreet bone in his body, Nathaniel thought as he looked over at Aaron. Great, he thought, now the master was grinning. As soon as he possibly could, Nathaniel was going back to Virginia where he felt safe and sane.

"Did either of you gentlemen see her mark? I'm to understand that it is unusual. I have a book here of other sigils that I've been collecting and wondered if you could look these over and let me know if you remember what it may have looked like?" a very nice-looking man said as he moved toward Nathaniel. The book looked ancient.

"Dad, what if it's her? What if she's come back after all this time?" the woman asked of the man who spoke. Nathaniel wondered why they cared about his mate. Then he shook himself mentally. She was not his mate, damn it.

"Who are you people and what does this mark have to do with Tess?"

"I'm sorry, Nathaniel Tremont, this is my mate and love, Sara. This is James and Savannah, and Phillip and Elizabeth. James and Savannah are Mel's parents. And Phillip and Elizabeth are Sara's grandparents. Mel is the current Queen of Magic."

These people knew something and he was willing to bet that they were also the ones Tess was running from. It was time to either cut his losses and leave before it was too late or stay and figure her out. His mind told him to get out, but his body was telling him to stay, that he would never get this chance again.

"Before I look in this book and tell you what I saw, maybe someone should tell me why it's important to you all. Why you're upset Tess left before you got to talk to her, and why she is running from you?"

"Nathaniel is right. He has a right to know. She is his mate, after all. Let's all adjourn to our house where we will be more comfortable. And we'll tell him everything we know. You will ride back with Sara and me. I'm sure you have questions," the master said.

Nathaniel had spent the daylight hours in the mansion. It was a lovely house full of antiques. There was also a beautiful blending of the old with the new. He had not had a chance to meet Aaron's family; it had been late when he had arrived and he had gone straight to the room Duncan had led him too. Now that he had met Sara he could see parts of her throughout the house and in the lair where he had slept.

An hour later they were sitting in the living room of the mansion. Duncan was walking around with a large tray of different types of food for the rest of the group while Nathaniel and Aaron waited until everyone settled.

Nathaniel was introduced to the alpha's mate, Alastriona, and to Bradley's two cubs, Charlie and Charlotte. When the children went off to play with Aaron's two children, the adults settled down to talk.

"Fifteen years ago, Sherman, my mate, tried to have me put to fade. Our kind can't die as we are true immortals, but we can fade from this realm into the next. I was nearly to term with our child, but she was killed in the explosion—not having her first breath, she was not yet like me, a true immortal. Sherman wanted to take over the realm and run it as he wanted and I was…I was in his way. Sara was the head of my Brianal Guard then and she and her guard were present at the time, having come to arrest him. She was able to get me out and put in a safe place. The other men, my Brianal Guards who followed Sara, were killed." Mel started the tale. "It took me years to recuperate from the injuries and the miscarriage. Then nearly three years passed before I was able to contact Sara again, and another year before I could tell my family where I was. Because I feared, without my full strength to fight him, he would succeed."

"If you can't die then what purpose did it serve to only put you into fade? What sort of magic did he use to overpower you? Just using black magic wouldn't do the amount of damage you're talking about. And wouldn't you have still been queen?" Nathaniel asked her.

"It was black magic and I've never been able to figure out who his trainer was. As for me being queen, that would be yes and no. Sherman would have been able to run the realm in my stead as my mate. But without my magic he would never be able to use his own. I am magic, black or white. This would have drained the realm, causing more damage than you can fathom. See, Nathaniel, black magic isn't a renewable source. It only takes from the things around it and never returns anything back. White magic, or pure magic, is clean and if used correctly can be used for other things. For example, the fairies of the forest wake the buds on the flowers with a kiss each morning. And every morning with the kiss, color is painted into the petals, dew is laid heavily on the blooms for their first drinks, and the sun nurtures them to open fully. When the flower dies, its roots continue to feed the soil, the blossoms and the petals fertilize the ground, and the color goes into the root systems for the trees to use in the fall. Understand?"

"Okay, so you have perpetual motion in magic. I understand, but not what this has to do with Tess. You said she was coming back, back from where?"

"Two weeks before Mel was hurt Tess came to me and told me that Sherman was going to harm Mel and their babe. Tess had details, information she said she got from his mind. As a Brianal Tess couldn't read Sherman's mind. But she had, she did. She also told me that he had plans to take over the realm and destroy the magic. None of us believed her. Well, that's not really true; we chose not to believe her. Tess was denounced as a member of the Brianal Guard and her immortality was revoked and she was reduced to only a fae because her actions were seen as crimes against the queen," Sara said.

"So, she was right. Everything she told you came to head and it happened just like she said. But that's not all, is it? Something else happened and now you are looking for her. What was it? Why are you so hot to speak to her?"

"Her family was a part of my guard. Her great-grandfather, grandfather, and father, they were all there with me. They were killed too. Sherman called out their names one at a time and took their immortality as he held them down with his magic. When the bomb when off, and because they were unable to leave, they died."

Christ, Nathaniel thought, her entire family gone because no one would listen to her, believe in her. But that still did not explain why they wanted to talk to her, seemed to need to talk to her. Unless…

"You don't know if this Tess is the one you're looking for, do you? That's what the book is for, so you can see if the woman you're chasing is the one you betrayed."

Nathaniel heard the hiss of anger from Aaron and he felt the anger surge through the room, but he was not here to make friends. He was here to try and understand the woman who went to the bank to borrow enough money to get transportation and ended up saving the bank untold amounts of money, both in money stolen and lawsuits, in the aftermath of all the probable deaths. "She knows you're chasing her; she even said that she wants nothing to do with you. So, what is it you want with her?"

"To ask her to forgive me, to forgive us. And to reinstate her to whatever level she wants. Give her whatever she wants," Mel said to him. He could hear the sincerity in her voice.

Nathaniel did not think Tess would want anything from these people, but he really did not know her that well. He did know that she was something of an enigma, not only to him, but to these people as well.

He walked over, picked up the book, and sat down with it. The first few pages were drawings of detailed sigils that were marked as Brianal. Each drawing bore the name of the person who wore it and other names had been added in a different hand. Then there was the significance of the design. Each person brought to the next design their own bit of it. Sara bore the mark of a Brianal, but hers differed in that she also carried the mark of the Brianal Guard.

He turned two more pages and saw a part of the mark Tess carried. The next page carried a bit more and the ninth page carried the last. He showed his findings to Phillip and knew that even they did not know what she carried, nor why.

"This mark here, the Brianal Guard, it has a black mark through the middle of it. The last mark is not black, but in all sorts of colors. It has a gold band around it at the bottom; it seems to go completely around her bicep."

"This is the mark of the Brianal Guard; we knew she had this one. The black mark was put to it when she was striped. Once Mel gives her part of the ritual, the black mark will disappear with her reinstatement. The second mark is of her fae heritage and her lineage. It signifies that she is a warrior fae. Her family has been fighting and protecting the Brianal Court since magic was first used. The last is a surprise. I don't think I've seen this mark since...well, I actually don't remember when. This is the mark of the Black Knights."

Chapter Four

Tess walked toward the bar. She tended there three nights a week for the extra cash. The place was in a horrible location, but the owner was a good friend and she liked helping him out.

Her belly was still tender. She knew that it was not really healed, but it had to do for now. She thought of the man who had healed her and then of the kiss.

Her body shuddered at the thought of the way his mouth fit over hers, the way his tongue slid along hers. Heat from him still warmed her, made her feel things she had not felt in centuries.

Opening the door to the bar, she stood until her eyes adjusted to the sudden darkness. This was by far the weirdest place she had ever worked.

There were the usual mixed drinks and beers on tap. The bar did not own a blender, so fruity drinks and daiquiris were not on the menu. The long bar had some stools, but mostly it catered to the people who stood near it. It was not a place with a lot of ambience; they served liquor.

"'Bout time, bitch. I told you to be here three minutes ago. You know how much I hate to be put off."

"Fuck off, you old fairy. I'll be here when you see me fucking walk in the door and not a minute before."

When Roger Clement scooped her up into a big bear hug, she squealed. This was a greeting that they had been doing since they met some two hundred years ago.

Roger was fae, not a warrior fae like her, but the normal, run of the mill type—if they tended to run near the three hundred pound area and were almost eight feet tall, that is. They had met when she was just a trainee in her father's troop.

Roger, thank goodness, had found her just after she had been told that her family was dead fifteen years ago and she had been a little out of her mind with grief. He and his family had been looking for her for several days, having just found out about the murders themselves.

Her rage was palatable and Roger had let her beat on him until she fell over from exhaustion. They had both taken and given a few punches before it was over. Then he had picked her up, gave her a good shake, and took her to his home to heal. It was there that she met Athropos, Clothos, and Lachesis; the Sisters Three, or the Fates.

When she had awakened they were in her room talking about her. And Roger was lying on the bed with her.

When she turned to glare at him he just grinned and ran his finger down her arm. "Don't worry your pretty little head, warrior. You are not my type and you well know it. I prefer my lovers to have much more equipment below the waist than you currently have. And the more, the better, if you know what I mean." He wiggled his brows at her and she could not help but laugh.

"Good. You're awake." One of them, Clothos Tess found out later, said as she sat on the bed too. "How are you feeling? Better, I hope. We're sorry about your loss. We loved your family very much. We're the Fates, Tess, and have a need for your services. You will begin working for us as soon as we can get a blade made for your size. I've never met a woman who was your height before. Anyway, when the blades are done, we'll begin your training."

"No. I don't want to work for any more otherworldly beings. But thanks for asking. Wait, you didn't, so never mind. I appreciate you taking me in, fae, but I have to get going. My grandmothers will need me."

"Your paternal family dying was a necessity, Tess. Their deaths will be avenged, I promise. You're going to get through this, but we are in need of your services now," Athropos said sadly.

"A necessity for whom? You? The queen? I tried to tell her and she wouldn't listen to me. My family would be alive today if she had gotten her head out of her ass and did what she promised. But she was too in love with that mate of hers to listen. Now look, they're all dead."

"So is her child, her daughter. She was tricked like all the others. You were not. That is why we need you. Black magic doesn't touch you. And because of that, you will lead our army of warriors. The Black Knights."

"No. I have things I want to do. I've been a guard for too long and I want to live my life for a change."

"I'm afraid you have no choice in the matter, Tess. You have been chosen," Athropos said just before she had touched Tess and burned the mark into her arm.

That had been fifteen years ago. Fifteen years of fighting wars with other beings, fifteen years of strife and death. Fifteen years of bringing order to the realm she had once vowed to detest. Tess had been working to keep the peace in Melody's realm and the queen was not aware of who it was that kept her safe.

The Fairy Queen, the bar she worked, was busy for a Wednesday night. Tess mixed drinks from five o'clock until eleven without stopping. She decided she needed a breath of fresh air and walked outside to get it.

Tess felt him the moment she shut the door behind her. Damn it all to hell and back, she thought. Why did this man keep showing up when she had no way to run?

"Whatever you want, I don't want it, I can't afford it, and it's too fattening anyway. Go away," she said to Nathaniel as she turned to go back inside.

"We never finished our talk. You…sidetracked us. I wanted to know what you knew about the men in the bank." He stepped out of the shadows and began walking toward her. He was so beautiful.

Nathaniel's light hair looked bright in the moonlight, highlighting the streaks of gold and red. His eyes looked black in the night until he got closer, then they became as brilliant and bright as a summer sky. Looking into them sent shivers down her spine. When he smiled—which had not been much when she was around—his teeth gleamed brightly in the moonlight. His mouth, she knew, was not as soft as it looked, but it was no less delicious tasting. His full lips were sensual and fit nicely over hers when he had kissed her. The width of his shoulders was wide and she could see herself hanging onto them when he took her.

Even at her height he still towered over her a good four inches, making her feel delicate and tiny when he was standing close. His cock was long and thick and her mouth watered when she thought of it pressed against her again as he had done this morning. Need rippled through her and she did not want to think about what they could do to one another if they were to let loose.

As much as she wanted to tease him again she knew that doing so now would not end with just a kiss, but with him taking her, taking her hard against the wall, on the ground, and against any surface that would hold them. Drawing in a shaky breath she realized that he was standing a mere foot away from her and she wanted him as badly as he wanted her.

"You should go. I have to work and you are…you're a distraction I don't need right now," she said, and hated the way her voice sounded breathy and soft.

"You've been a distraction to me since I inhaled your scent again a few days ago. I can't think about anything but having you. I want to be inside of you, deep and hard. I want to fuck you until neither of us can walk then lay you down and fuck you again. No amount of jerking off has relived the thought of you taking me into your mouth, my coming down the back of your throat while you swallow every drop of me. I want to pull your nipples into my mouth and suckle them until you come, then I want to lick your clitoris over and over until you have filled me with your cum. Christ, Tess, I've never wanted a woman as badly as I do you." He ground his hard cock into her, taking her breath away in the process.

His dark, heavy voice made her wet; his words made her wetter. When she put out her hands to push him away and go into the bar, he pulled her close and kissed her.

His mouth did not kiss as much as take; he did not take so much as conquer; he did not conquer so much as claim.

She knew that he was moving them, taking them somewhere other than outside of the bar. When she felt the mattress touch the back of her legs she let him lead her down to it and cover her with his body. She could not think beyond having him touch her, his bare skin moving along hers.

His mouth never left hers, but their hands were no less busy. As he opened her thighs and pressed between them she ran her nails down his back and grabbed at his shirt to pull it up over his head. Breaking the kiss long enough to remove his shirt, he took the sides of her tee, ripped it open and then did the same to her bra. Her breasts bounced with the movement and he watched them with hunger in his eyes.

Standing now, he looked down at her and smiled, his fangs long and his eyes dark with need. Licking her lips, she looked up at him and ran her finger down his erection before she looked back up at his eyes.

"Take off your pants for me, agent. I want to see your cock before you bury it in me." He groaned and started to unbuckle his belt. His movements were slow and deliberate. He was teasing her and she was too needy to appreciate it.

Sitting up, she moved his hands and began working the buttons on his jeans open and kissed each inch of his skin as she exposed it. His hard cock lay to the side and working her finger over the rigid shaft, she moved it to the opening of his pants. When it was where she wanted it, she pulled his briefs down and licked the purple head as she continued to open the last button.

"Christ, woman. Your mouth needs to take me, now."

Moving the pants down over his ass and just below his balls, she cupped him from the rear and opened her mouth wide over him, taking him into her heat.

He was so wide she could barely hold him all, and the crown was so thick. Pulling back she heard him growl, but wanted to taste all of him and licked her way down his vein to the dark nest of curls. She had shown him this in her thoughts and did not realize how well she had imagined him.

His fingers laced in her hair and she felt him guide her back to the head. The stream of pre cum nearly had her come with anticipation and she lapped it into her mouth with a hungry suckle. He tasted like his blood; hot, spicy, and hers.

Wrapping her hand around him, she began to pump him hard as she took him into her mouth again. Over and over she swirled her tongue over him, teasing the tiny eye with the tip, moaning when she felt more of him spill into her.

"I want to come here, come down your throat, but I want to feel your body come all over my cock too. Stop now, baby, before I spill my seed this way."

Reluctantly she took her mouth off his cock and lapped once more at the head for another taste. She lay back on the bed when he reached down and took off her jeans. When she was naked he stood over her and looked at every inch of her.

"You're beautiful. I don't know if I can be gentle this time. My need to be in you is overwhelming. I want to fuck you until you scream, till we both scream."

"Do it. Fuck me hard, Nathaniel. Please." She opened her legs wide and let him see how badly she wanted him; her pussy was drenched and needy. Reaching down, she opened her nether lips wider and began to play with her clit while he watched. She knew she was only making him harder, but Christ, she thought, her body needed to come.

She felt him move her hands and, before she could sit up to see what he was doing, his tongue pushed inside of her. Suckling him for those precious few moments and then playing with herself had made her too close and his tongue threw her into a tailspin and out of control.

"Nathaniel!" she screamed as she came, her hips bucked, nearly knocking him off her. Panting hard and wanting more she grabbed a handful of his hair and pulled him up her and to her mouth. Even as he settled his cock at her entrance, she wrapped her legs around his hips and surged up, hard and fast. He slammed into her as she rocked up again. She came again, her body tightening around his thickness; the pain/pleasure of him being so long and wide was amazing.

Rocking into her again, she felt him still for a moment then rock again, harder this time as he came inside of her. Over and over he pulsed his hot cum into her; over and over he said her name as he did.

Finally, he collapsed on top of her. And just when she thought he was getting too heavy he rolled to his back, taking her with him.

She sat up slightly, almost too tired to move, and looked at him. His fangs were biting into his lower lip. She could tell that he was hungry, his need to feed from her as strong to her as if she was the needy one. She would feed him like this, the ability to mate now over as they were no longer coming.

"You didn't feed. You didn't feed from me when you came to the bar. I can feel your hunger." She started to move up his chest to have him bite her, but his next words froze her in place.

"I didn't want to. We're not going to become mated or bonded vamps. This will be enough for me until I have to go back to Virginia."

Chapter Five

Nathaniel woke and could not remember where he was for a few seconds. The room was black as pitch and he could not make out anything familiar. Finally, he remembered that he had gone to see Tess and had ended up back here in his bed. Smiling, he settled back on the bed to reach for Tess.

She was gone. And she had been gone for some time, as the sheets were cold and the room was chilled. Reaching out to find her he met with a hard wall and frowned.

Picking up his cell phone he saw that he had two missed calls and a message. Turning on the bedside light, he dialed voicemail.

"It's Tess. I'm going back to work. Then tomorrow I'm going to my other place for a few weeks. I guess we won't see each other before you leave. It's been great. Well, bye, and thanks for the good time."

He pulled the phone from his ear and stared at the thing before he redialed the message again. "Thanks for the good time?" What the hell was that supposed to mean?

He tried to reach her again and hit the same wall. He opened his phone to see if she left a phone number from however she had called him and realized that she had used a landline to call him from. And if his memory was correct, she had used the one in this room to leave him the message.

"Damn it!" Before he threw the phone across the room he set it gently on the bedside table and got up to pace, trying to remember what he might have done.

They had had sex, but that couldn't be it—unless he had hurt her. He didn't think he had, but if he had, then she should have said something to him, not run away. But he didn't think that was it. Rubbing his hand over his face, he tried to think. They hadn't said anything before going to bed. He realized he was grinning and tried to stop it, but found he could not. They had been animals for each other. Sobering, he realized that this was not helping him figure out why she had left without as much as a goodbye.

Well, he thought, that wasn't true either; she had left him a message. "Thanks for the good time" message. He got mad all over again, showered, and got dressed.

Maybe Duncan or one of the others in the household had seen her and knew where she had gone. He just hoped he didn't see the master of the house on his way out. Maybe he should just leave and not ask.

Walking into the kitchen, he knew he should have taken his own advice and left the moment he saw them all in the kitchen. It did not improve his mood, nor curb his tongue, when he noticed that they were smiling and seemingly having a good time.

"Where is she? Tess, where is she?" he demanded as he opened the door.

Aaron merely raised a brow, but Sara got mad and while she did not yell, her voice conveyed her anger as nothing else might have. "People do not growl in my house, especially guests. You want something, you ask politely or not at all.

Now, you walk out that door and come back in and be nice about it."

He stared at her for a few seconds then turned around to go back out. He was leaving and there was not a damned thing these people could do about it. Sara's next statement whispering through his mind had him stopping in his tracks.

"You leave this house like this and I will hunt you down, castrate you, serve up your dick with your mashed balls on a platter, and make you eat it. I'm in no mood to fuck with you today so I would suggest you gird up your manhood and do what I told you. If you don't believe I have it in me to do just what I said, then try me."

Closing his eyes, he turned back around, stepped into the kitchen, and smiled. It might not have reached his eyes, but it was the best he could do under the circumstances. "Good morning. I was wondering if anyone might have noticed where Tess might have disappeared to this morning. I'm not positive when she left, but it would have been sometime after two this morning."

"Much better, not perfect, but we'll work on your delivery later. She wasn't here when I got up at four so I think your timeline is correct. Did she leave angry?"

Nathaniel sat down and looked over at Aaron. He knew he was going to regret this, but the look on his face was more than he could bear. "What?"

"I thought you weren't going to mate with her. Her scent is all over you, by the way. I don't believe you bonded, but you should be able to find her without blood. She does have yours. If she is half as angry as you are, this might prove to be fun."

"She's blocking me. And I have no intent…ah fuck! I told her that. I told her that we weren't going to bond, that the sex would be enough until I left again. Shit! No wonder she left without a word. Damn it. What the fuck else could go wrong?"

The giggling children had him flush with embarrassment. He had forgotten about them and looked over at Sara. If he was honest with himself, he was more afraid of her than her mate. She just looked like she could take him on and win. And he did not trust her smile right now.

"I'm sorry, mistress. I'm not…it's been a very long time since I've been around civilized people and longer still since I've been around children. The men I work with, well, we don't exactly get invited to many tea parties in our line of work. I'm not even sure that most of them would know a tea cup anyway. Forgive me."

"No, I don't imagine you do. The children have heard that particular word a time or two before, haven't they, Aaron love?"

The large vamp, master of his own realm, overlord to several thousand vamps, dropped his head and nodded. Nathaniel was not sure, but he thought he might have seen a hint of a smile on his face before he lifted his head up again and winked at the children.

Nathaniel was sure this was the strangest house he had ever been in and also the most loving. He was suddenly glad that he had taken Aaron up on his "suggestion" to come stay at the mansion. He really had not been around anyone that did not drop the "F" bomb every other word and quite a few more just as colorful.

"Master Nathaniel, if you do not mind my buttering in, but did Lord Phillip not mention that she was a Black Knight? I'm sure they have their little get-togethers somewhere, and that someone would know where they are. I could ask Miss Mel. She may have a YPM to find those type of meetings."

Nathaniel looked at Sara and then at Aaron; confusion marred both their faces. Buttering in? YPM? He was about to ask Duncan what he meant by YPM when Lizzy spoke up.

"Mr. Duncan, it's GPS not YPM. Remember? Aunt Pete told you that last week when she tried to show you how to use it in the car."

"How did that go, the teaching, Lizzy?" Sara asked. Nathaniel looked up at her sharply and noticed she was nearly cross-eyed trying not to laugh. He wondered if this was a normal thing, Mr. Duncan messing up a phrase. Then Nathaniel remembered that Duncan had told him that the lair was specially booted to keep others out.

"He's hopeless, she said. She said that he is the only man she had ever met that could get lost in the garage walking from one car to the next. I think I know why he called it YPM, though. She told him that she put the GPS in his car to help him with 'your puny memory.' She kept saying that over and over to him. I thought it was funny, but Aunt Pete said that Mr. Duncan had a handicap. I asked her what that meant and she said never mind."

"She most certainly did not say I had a puny anything, young lady. She said it was to help me with my negative sense of direction. I like that so much better than puny memory. Miss Pete said that I was her favorite trainee."

"Yeah, but Mr. Duncan, you're her only trainee, aren't you?" Mac asked with all seriousness.

"Yes, I am, so that does make me her favorite, does it not? Would you like another scone, Lady Sara? I believe Miss Penny has some fresh ones in the pantry for you."

Aaron was fighting his mirth; Nathaniel could see it, but Sara was nearly falling off her chair with laughter. The children just continued to eat their breakfast as though nothing at all was wrong with their parents.

Yeah, Nathaniel thought, the strangest household he had ever been in.

~~~
~~~

“Give! I give. Please, no more. I give, my lady.”

Tess was breathing hard; sweat poured from her body in wide streams. Pushing her soaked hair out of her eyes, she looked down at the man on the ground and the blood on his tunic—lots of blood. She started to reach for him and he scrambled away from her on his knees. She took a step back then another and backed into her second in arms, Albadar.

“You keep this up and you’ll kill them, wear them all out to the point of uselessness, or terrify them so much they land on a sword to keep from disappointing you. This is the fourth man you’ve taken down today. How about you give me a go?”

His sword was suddenly in front of him. Before she could raise hers, he swiped at her quickly, slicing a long mar along her bicep. He did not break the skin, but the red scratch was there for all to see.

“You too tired to fight someone with better skills or are you too frightened of my superiority?” He swiped again, but this time, she was ready. His blade met with steel, not skin.

“No, not tired. I figured that I’m just about ready for you now. The others have taken the edge off and I won’t hurt you so badly now that some of my energy has dissipated.” Her blade whistled through the air and landed on his arm just where he had scratched her, but she drew blood. “First blood, you owe me a boon.”

“The only one you’ll get this day, master. The only one.”

For the next hour and a half, they fought. Not a soul on the field did anything but marvel at the pair as they fought and bantered. Blade against blade, matched perfectly when one of them was not trying to fight a demon within, but anger fueled Tess and time and time again she bit into Albadar’s skin with her sword. Their insults and laughter fought hard to be heard over the clanging of steel hitting steel.

Albadar managed to draw second blood, but he never got close enough again to lay his sword against her skin. Several times she nearly went too deep with her blade, but he never called "give," the word they used to stop when it became too much or one was too exhausted to go on. She, however, managed to cut him eight more times before they were called to halt by the arrival of Athropos, one of the Fates.

"Mistress, if you could give us but a few minutes, we'll get cleaned up and meet you in the dining hall. I'm sure this one has built up quite the appetite. She has managed to take down four of her own men today without so much as an apple to fortify her." Albadar playfully punched at Tess's chin and grinned.

"Yes. My sisters are on their way and this will give them time to get here. Take your time, you know how they are, always late for everything."

"Thank you, we won't be long." Tess started to turn away, but Athropos stopped her with a hand on her arm.

"You've met your match. Good. That will make things so much easier for you from now on. I'm happy for you, Tess."

Tess did not understand the statement, but it mattered little anyway. So she pulled loose, started walking backwards away from her and answered. "He said he doesn't want me. He'll be going back to Virginia soon and I was just someone to fuck. I have to get cleaned up; I'll meet you in the house in a few." Turning around, she had to keep herself from running as fast as she could away from her.

Tess got to her house without anyone stopping her. She was pretty sure that word had gotten around that she was quite mad, what with her taking down four of her own men and the manic way she had been doing things this past week. Laughing slightly, she thought maybe she was.

She was angry with herself for letting Nathaniel's rejection of her color her ability to do her job. More so because she did not know why it bothered her that he had. She did not want or need a mate any more than he did, obviously. She did all right on her own. But he had rejected her and it did hurt. Turning off the water, she started to get dressed and was stunned by what she saw in the mirror.

Tess doubted there was one square inch of her body that was not covered in a bruise or cut. Christ! She looked like a Jackson Pollack painting, bright colors of red and blue here, darker browns and blacks there in between the bright white of unmarred skin. Even the sigils on her arm were unnoticeable due to the massive bruise on her shoulder.

Pulling on a pair of jeans and a long-sleeved shirt to cover most of the marks, she left her house and made her way to the large dining house, plaiting her hair into a tight braid as she went.

The main hall was a massive room filled with table after table, each with twelve chairs around it. There were currently over three hundred men and women under her command and she made it a point to make sure they all ate at least one meal together when they could. Dinner was this week, so when she walked in every solider stood and saluted her with their blades. Nodding, she walked to the back of the line to get her meal.

The Sisters and Albadar were already at one table and they had saved a seat for her across from them. She picked up her sandwich and bit down into the veggie sub. She did not eat meat often and preferred chicken to anything else. With her mouth full, she looked at Lachesis and grinned. "Hungry."

"So I see. Albadar tells me you've been working rather hard at something. Or are you working hard to understand something? Want to talk about it?"

"No. And stay out of my head. You came here for a reason, and I'm sure it wasn't for the special. Spill it."

"Always straight to the point, aren't you? All right. First, we need to talk about Nathaniel," Clotho demanded.

"No and hell no. Next topic. And if you bring him up again, I'm out of here. I have more important things to do than talk about a vampire and what he may or may not be to me. Frankly, I think it's a moot point, so let's move on, shall we? You said there was an issue coming up we may have to deal with. Do you have any more information about that?"

"Albadar, could you be a dear and go away? We need to talk with Tess about something and if you are sitting too close she may hurt you again. You know how she can be when she gets pissy."

"Very funny, Athropos. You should have gone into show business. And I do not get pissy. I get pissed. Big difference. If you ladies are quite through, I have things to do." She stood to go.

"Sit down." The command in her voice made it so that Tess could do nothing but obey Athropos. She sat.

The Sisters Three as a whole was who Tess worked for. But Athropos was the one who actually commanded her. She had been the one to touch Tess's arm and burn the sigil into her skin. She was also the only one who could remove it.

Tess had been recruited to command the Black Knights, an elite group of immortal men and women who guarded the realm and had been doing so since magic had first started being used by outsiders of the magical realm. She had agreed to lead the men rather than merely train them as she had been "recruited" to do from the start, gaining their respect as well as their loyalty. Any one of them would die for her, and she for them.

"What did he say to you that lead you to believe that he didn't want you, Tess? You may have read too much into it. I have heard of men saying things in the heat of the moment that they would normally never say to someone they love."

"He doesn't love me, nor do I love him. I offered him my throat and he said that we he didn't want to feed from me, that we weren't going to become a bonded couple. He said that the sex we had just had would be enough for him until he had to go back to Virginia. Pretty sure there was nothing there I could read into other than what he it sounded like. He was serious and I left."

"Have you tried to talk to him since then? Of course you haven't, I can tell by the look on your face. You are so…how long have you been here since then? It couldn't be much more than twenty-four hours."

"Five days ago. Why? What possible reason could you have for caring what happens to me sexually? It's not like I was a virgin. I knew what I was getting into when I fucked him."

"Don't be crude. And has he tried to contact you in any way? Or have you closed down that vault you call a mind from him? Have you thought of the consequences of you shutting him out?"

"Again, why is it any of your business what happens to me? I've given you no reason to think that I want a deep and lasting friendship. You're my boss. I do my job for you, the one you hired me for. Stay out of my personal life."

"I would love to be more than your 'boss,' as you call it, but you're still pissed off I asked you to become a part of the Black Knights. Besides, I'm afraid that isn't possible for us to stay out, not now." They both looked up when Albadar and another man walked toward them. "Thank you, Albadar.

Please have a seat, Agent Tremont. Tess and I were just discussing your role in her life as a mate."

Chapter Six

"My lady, the demon lord Marlus would like a word. He is claiming that it is within his rights to claim your kingdom," the aide, Chantal, said.

"How is it within his…you know, I don't care. Send him away." Mel was tired and she was worried about Tess. The stupid woman blocked her at every turn. Mel had hoped that with Tess having a mate now it would be easier for her to finally get to talk to her, but it seemed she was just as elusive.

"My lady, I don't think that is such a good idea. He is quite persistent in his need to speak with you. He claims that you are an unbound woman without a descendent and he has the Council's backing on this. I believe you should let him speak."

Mel looked away from her aide. It would not due to have Chantal see the queen cry, Mel thought. And why today, of all days, did Marlus have to come by and talk about her not having a child?

This week marked the anniversary of the death of her little girl. It had been fifteen years. Mel wondered what she would have been like, what she may have looked like. It was depressing to her to think how much she had lost in just seconds. Taking a deep breath, Mel turned back to her friend and aide, Chantal.

"Tell him to give me thirty minutes and then contact my mother and grandmother. If you can also get Sara here, I would be very grateful. Did he say which member of the Council he had backing from?"

"Yes, my lady, all of them. I will see what I can do about your family. And I will have Marshall bring in tea and cakes. I believe that the demon is allergic to the tea."

Mel was still grinning when her mother came in ten minutes later. Sometimes humor came at the most unexpected times, she thought, as she hugged her mom.

"Chantal tells me that Marlus is up to his old tricks again. That man has a lot of nerve. You know he tried this same trick on me when I was in labor with you. He told the Council that I was incapacitated and should I die during the birth he was more than willing to step in and take over. I thought your father was going to cut his throat. Of course we had to tell the simpleton that our breed does not die. I hope he has the balls to not wear long sleeves. I gave him quite a mark the last time he was here. See if you can read his tat."

"Oh, Mom. He may have a valid point this time. He is correct in what he's saying. I am unbound and childless. Chantal said that he has the backing of the entire Council on this."

"Poppycock. That man will suffer greatly for his stupidity. What are you going to do?"

"See him. He should be here in about ten minutes. Where's Grandma? I'd like to face him with full force."

"She and your grandfather are on another honeymoon. If you ask me, I think they are the horniest people I've ever met. Good heavens! They go at it as much as Sara and that Aaron do. Why, I caught them doing it on the table the other morning. They are quite nimble for beings their age, I must say."

"Mother. Remember the rules? You are never to discuss your sex life, Grandma's sex life, or anybody else's sex life with me. I don't now, nor do I ever want to think about any one of you having sex in any way, shape, or form. Do I make myself clear?"

"Yes, darling. But how do you think…"

"No! Do not finish that sentence! Now. We are going to pretend that you and I were discussing the weather and then we'll let Marlus in. All right?"

"I didn't know that I had such a prude as a daughter. But all right, if it helps you to sleep at night, then we won't discuss how you were conceived. We found you under a rock. Is that better?"

"Yes. Yes, I believe it is. Now, what do I do with Marlus?"

"Fuck him?"

Mel shuddered and walked to her throne room. Some days, like today, she felt all of her forty-five hundred years. She decided that as soon as possible, she was going to take a long vacation somewhere fun. Maybe she would go to Cedar Point. Duncan had told her he had had a great time there with Sara and the children last month. And the pictures he had shown her looked fun. She remembered fun, sort of.

Marlus walked in just as Mel and her mother sat down. Sara had said she would be there in a jiffy, whatever that was, and to not do anything stupid until Sara could bail her out. Mel snorted. As if she would, she thought.

"Marlus, would you like some tea?" He backed away from the tray as if it had been a snake. Mel sat down with another smile. "I'd like to know what you think you're doing. You've come to take my kingdom, have you? Molavonta is not up for discussion. I'm the ruler of this realm and all the realms surrounding it. Magic is mine, not to be bartered with by the likes of you."

"My queen, I only have the people's best interest at heart. They need a sovereign that will make sure the rules are followed. How do you expect them to follow you when you can't even abide by them yourself? You are in violation of the laws set forth by your liege. I demand that you yield to me and no one will get hurt."

"You dare threaten me? You will leave this castle and never return, Marlus, or so help me, I will hurt you in ways you cannot imagine. I am the queen. You will leave on your own or I will call my guard and have you thrown out."

Marlus moved so quickly that Mel had no opportunity to defend herself. He was behind her with a blade at her throat and her mother across the floor in a heap in seconds, tossed there by his magic.

"We could deal well, you and me, Melody," Marlus whispered in Mel's ear. "You agree to be my mate and I will make sure that you are taken well care of, your family as well. Say yes and I will become your king and you may rule behind me. Think of the magic you and I together could make." He ran his hand over her breast and squeezed hard. She felt her stomach roll with nausea.

Mel felt the power surge in the room seconds before Sara appeared. Even dressed in jeans and a t-shirt, Sara was a warrior. Putting out her hand, a bolt of magic shot forward and into Marlus, hitting him hard in the shoulder. He stumbled, but did not lessen his grip on Mel's neck.

"Let her go and we won't kill you," Sara said with steel in her voice.

"We? You seem to be quite alone, Sara dear. Has being mated to a vamp made you dumber? I will have what I want, it was promised to me. I'm merely here to offer my dear queen a deal."

"Promises, schomises. Perhaps you should take another look, Marlus."

Aaron appeared first, his eyes bright red with his anger, his fangs biting deep into his lower lip, then Colin, Tucker, and Dominic, all vampires ready to do battle armed with their swords, knives, and magic. The room shimmered and pulsed with it. Eliz and Phillip were next, and James brought up the rear. Mel smiled wildly at her family. She had never been so glad to see anyone as she was these people.

Mel felt Marlus stiffen behind her, his own power diminishing under the power of theirs. He took a step back and then another, still holding onto Mel as he went.

"This isn't over. I'll be back. And when I am, we will see who rules this land. Take this as my final warning, Melody, Mistress of the Light, Keeper of the Magick. The next time we meet, it will be while standing in your blood."

Mel felt herself being tossed forward and, before she could turn, Marlus was gone. She looked up at her family. They could not win, she thought. He would take her kingdom and kill them all. Because without the magic of Molavonta and the hold she had over it Mel and her family were just as mortal as any human.

~~~

"You can't be serious. There is no way that you can make me bond with her. This is the most ridiculous thing I've ever heard."

Nathaniel was pissed. He had been asleep in his borrowed lair when suddenly his door burst open and a he had been snatched from the bed. And none too gently either. His shoulder still hurt from the bite of the blade one man held. He did smile, however; it had taken eight of them to haul him in.
~~~

"Oh, I'm very serious. You will bond with Tess. You should have done so already. You are not leaving here until you do. There are things set in motion and you two are to play an integral part in it."

Nathaniel looked at Athropos and then threw back his head and laughed. His humor was genuine. He wondered if she actually thought that it would be a hardship to stay. "Stay here forever? Let me see, I can see the sun without bursting into small bits, I can walk among beings I've only ever read about, the weather is warm, and I never get hungry. Not really a great incentive to comply with your demands, is it? No. I choose my own future and I will not allow you or anyone else to tell, no, demand that I take a mate. So, if there is nothing else…" He stood to go.

"Sit down, Nathaniel, I'm not finished. You will take Tess as your mate or I will kill her. Right now, this very moment, I will cut her thread and she will be dead. That is the only choice you have. I'm not messing around with you two any longer."

"Then kill me. I could care less. I won't be mated to a man who does not want me and vise versa. You've taken everything I've ever cared about from me, so killing me is fine. I will even lend you the blade to do it."

Nathaniel watched as Tess stopped her pacing, reached into her boot, pulled out a long, thin blade, and threw it across the long room.

End over end it went and then landed with a snap an inch from the sandaled toes of Athropos. The blade quivered for several seconds as he stared at it, Tess and Athropos never taking their eyes from one another. He swallowed hard. She had never looked where she was throwing the knife and knew where it would land precisely.

Athropos looked over at Nathaniel then at Tess who had not moved from her stance. Without taking her eyes from Tess,

Athropos pulled the blade out of the floor and walked toward her. Magic churned from her empty hand as she walked, and suddenly there was a long thread in her hand. It trailed the floor as it lengthened as Athropos continued to Tess.

"You have lived a long life, child, and it could have been much longer. I do not like threats. And I feel that rather than try to negotiate it is much easier just to cut my losses—no pun intended. Goodbye, love." The blade slipped into the loop that Athropos formed and she stiffened to pull the sharp point through it.

No, Nathaniel's mind screamed. "I'll do it. I'll bond with her. Just don't cut that cord." Nathaniel was just as surprised as the women appeared to be about what had spilled from his mouth. It was then that he realized he would do it; he would gladly bond with Tess rather than let her die. He could not let her die, not if he could do something about it.

"Well bully for you. But I said no. I won't have anyone who won't have me and I'm not particularly fond of either of you right now so forget it. I don't need anyone to sacrifice himself for me. Cut the fucking cord, Athropos. I've no use for your games either."

"If you lie to me, vamp, I will end you as well. If you say yes again, you will bond with her or I cut both your cords."

"I don't lie. I'll bond with her. She'll be my mate before the end of this day. I'll see to it."

Nathaniel held his breath as Tess turned to him. Not saying a word, she then turned to Athropos. She looked so hurt that he nearly reached out to pull her into his arms. But he knew that now would not be a good time to show her comfort. She would more than likely slit his throat than to have him touching her.

"If you do this, Athropos, I'll never forgive you. Never," Tess said. "And you know that I will hold true to this. This isn't right, not to him, nor to me, and you know it. "

"You will see that it will all work out as soon as you are bonded with him, child. I swear it. You must learn to trust me."

"Come on, Tess. Let's go. I made a promise and I intend to keep it." He had tried for humor, but failed miserably. Tess was hurt and angry and he did not like how it made him feel.

"I'm not going anywhere with you, so you can just—put me down, you moron. I will not mate or whatever with you."

Nathaniel was a little afraid of what she might do to him once he put her down, but for now he felt he was semi safe. He had thought picking her up and tossing her over his shoulder was a good idea until he realized where her teeth were. The second she sank her teeth into his ribs he wished he had thought of a different way of transporting her to her house.

"Ouch! Damn it, woman, you bite me again and I'll paddle your ass until you scream." He stopped suddenly, the image of that burning through his mind.

Christ. Her naked bottom lying across his thighs while he brought his hand down hard against it nearly made him groan out loud. The thought of her naked alone had him rock hard; her begging and wet over his cock made him lightheaded with need.

He had had to ask several men milling around where Tess's home was as she would not answer him. By the time he made it to the beautiful little house across the compound, he had quite a following. When he turned around at one point on the way across the road he noticed he had about fifty people right behind him.

They looked to be hard men, most dressed in armor of some sort. All of them carried a weapon—knives, swords, he'd even seen a couple of handguns as well. He somehow knew that the only reason he was not dead was because Athropos had given him a free pass. And if he did not follow through on his promise to her he would not be able to run far enough or hide deep enough where these men would not find him. Especially if he hurt Tess in any way.

When the door opened seconds before he stepped on the porch he knew that someone was making sure he at least got this far with the beautiful and thoroughly pissed off bundle in his arms. He did not have a lot of time to look around, but he had the impression of deep colors of the earth and plants everywhere. He took her to the bedroom and decided to try and set down some rules before he let the cat loose.

"If I put you down, will you try to hurt me?" he asked her.

"No, I won't try to hurt you; I am going to hurt you. First thing I'm going to do is rip your lips off, and then I'm going to tie you down and cut off that tiny dick of yours and give it to the dogs down the street."

His hand snapped across her ass so smartly that it stung his hand a bit. He could not imagine how it felt to her. His cock ached to see her naked ass pinked up, and it was everything he could do to restrain himself from finding out.

"First of all, I don't have a tiny dick, and secondly, you aren't helping yourself by making threats. Thirdly, I was thinking you might enjoy me tying you down. I would love to have you naked and tied open for me. It could be quiet enjoyable for us both."

"You try that and I'll…I'll…you'd better not try it."

Her arousal hit him fast and hard. With her positioned the way she was he could almost turn his nose into her pussy and breathe her in. Deciding maybe he could loosen her up a bit this way he sent her images of what he would do to her when he got her where he wanted her. He started to caress her inner thighs with his fingers, not touching, but coming close to her heat.

"I'd want you naked, your body bare of anything that would keep me from viewing you, touching you. I'd tie your arms high above your head, securing each wrist to the posts with silk, then your legs tied wide open for me, your pussy open for me. You'd be wet, soaking the sheets beneath you, all for me. Your scent is permeating the air and driving me wild with need. I want to taste of you, Tess."

"No. You're just horny. I'm sure there are plenty of women you can slake your need on. Why don't you put me down and go and find one?"

"No, darling, you're the one I want. I'd start with your breasts, working your nipples into hard peak and begging for my mouth. I'd lick them, first one then the other, not taking them into my mouth like I want, but just tasting them with my tongue. I'd move my way down your chest, nipping and kissing you as I go, tasting your sweat, your need as it glistened on your body. By the time I get to paradise you would be begging me to take you, begging me to pound my cock deep into your pussy. Is that what you want, Tess. Do you want me to fuck you?"

"Please, Nathaniel. Put me down." Her voice had turned soft and barely a whispered plea, and he heard her need within each word.

There was a moment when he wasn't sure if it was a trick and decided he didn't care. He wanted her and he could smell her need for him.

Adjusting her slightly, he pulled her slowly around him until her pussy was even with his mouth and he bit her through her pants, now soaked with her juices. He felt her fingers dig deep into his shoulders as she undulated her body. Sliding her down more, he took her breasts. His mouth opened over her and through her shirt he nibbled hard at the nipple he could feel pressing against her bra. His cock jerked in response and the need to smooth his hand over it, to calm his cock into waiting just a little while longer, made him groan out loud.

She was panting hard, as hard if not harder than him. By the time her feet touched the floor they were both tearing at their clothes and each other's. He felt his fangs elongate, stretch in his mouth, wanting—no, needing—to sink into her flesh and take.

Backing her toward her bed as soon as he had her bare from the waist up, he lifted her again, took her warm breast into his mouth and suckled hard, rolling her nipple against the roof of his mouth, tugging with his teeth. She bucked against him and moaned deep from her chest.

Working beneath her legs that were wrapped around his waist, he jerked the snap and zipper open on his pants and freed his cock. The cool breeze in the room made it ache all the more. Putting his hands into Tess's opened pants, he tore them from her. Her moan rippled through him like a caress.

"I need to be inside of you. I need to bury my cock deep into you, Tess."

"Nathaniel, this is wrong. You know it and I know it. You have to stop now before it's too late. We can have sex, but we shouldn't bond, not this way."

"I couldn't stop even if I wanted to. I want you, Tess. Now."

As soon as her back touched the bed, he was sliding into her, her juices making his entrance easy but no less tight. He wanted to slow down, he wanted to savor her and how much they fit together, but he could not. She was milking him, pulling and tugging around his cock so tightly that he knew he was close.

Licking her throat, running his tongue down her vein, he captured her pounding pulse in his mouth and suckled hard on it. The need to claim her nearly making him dizzy, his world suddenly focused on making her his, claiming his mate.

Lifting his head slightly, he looked down at her and he felt everything slow and calm within him. "Tess, I want you more than I've ever wanted anything in my life. I want taste you, take you as mine. And I give you all that I am. Please drink from me, claim me as I do you."

She looked up at him for so long that he began to get nervous. Just when he started to say something, he noticed the tears in her eyes.

"Don't do this, please? Don't bond with me, Nathaniel; it isn't right for us, not like this, not this way. Please, don't."

"I made a promise, Tess. Please, if we don't do this, she will kill you. She has the means and I don't want to take the chance that she will."

Tess turned her head away from him and bared her neck for him. He could see her tears running down her cheeks. He knew that he had put them there and his heart ached with the knowledge. But he knew that he could not lose her, not now, not like this. Licking the pulse again and rocking into her, he felt her tighten again around him, pulling him deeper into her. His balls drew up tight to his body and he knew that he would not last. Before he could change his mind, he bit.

Her essences filled his mouth, hot and spicy. When he drew hard on the vein, he came, his body releasing his hot seed into her, filling her, marking her as his. Her blood filled him. He could feel it surge into his vessels and cells, giving him the feeling of having just drank the finest wine and eaten the richest chocolate. Over and over he surged into her until he collapsed once again upon her. Dragging in an intoxicating breath of her, he pulled Tess over him as he rolled to his back and held her tight. Next time, he told himself, next time she would bond with him. And he fell into the deep sleep of his kind.

Chapter Seven

Tess stepped out into the sun and winced at the pain it caused her. She had been crying most of the night after Nathaniel fell asleep and only just now had been able to move his body off of hers. Her eyes were tender. He had been heavy and he kept pulling her back every time she got a few inches away.

He had done it. He had bonded with her and now he would need her to live. It hurt her in ways she could not imagine, him not listening to her. Did he not realize that she was a mortal and, with their bonding, he would share that? As a vampire he was immortal in that it was more difficult to be killed. The only thing she had going for her was her very long life. If hurt in any way, even in sickness, she would die.

Moving toward the paddock she met Lord Draco. He had just settled down near the deep lake to nap, as he did every day at this time, when she called out to him. "Hello, my lord. How are you feeling these days? You look better than the last time I saw you."

Lord Draco Enneahedral was a Ninefold dragon—one of the largest and oldest of his kind ever seen. He was also thought to be the last and that was why he lived in the magical realm now. He stood fifteen feet tall and, with his wingspan, he was thirty feet wide. When Tess stood close to his head one of his teeth was the same height as she was, yet she was never fearful of him or ever thought he would harm her. She loved the old guy.

"I am fine, my dear, and you? Is this not a glorious day? I thought I would try to catch a few winks before I go home and take a nap later," he whispered through her head.

He could not use his real voice when he was in his dragon form. It was hard and loud, and the last time he had used it the fairies had been upset for nearly a decade, refusing to kiss any flower in the field where he rested. The poor dragon had been so depressed he began to molt. It was a very sad time for all those who had to clean up after him. Scales were very heavy and could be quite sharp on the edges. She noticed that the field surrounding him was full of bluebell and marsh flowers of rich summer colors.

"I'm going to the Caves of Avalone for some peace and quiet. I haven't been there in a long while and thought that I would enjoy it for a little while. I think a few hours alone would do wonders for my aching head. I would ask that if anyone asks you if you have seen me that you tell them nothing."

"I will keep your secret, warrior. But let me ask, who do you run from, Tessa May Knight, the young vamp in your bed or from yourself? Both of them will still be there when you come back home, you know. It is better to deal with the issues at hand rather than put them off for another day. This is a lesson it took me many a year to figure out."

She did not want to know how he knew about the man in her bed or even how he knew that he was a vampire, but she knew that he was right. No matter how far she ran from the problems at hand they would still be there when she returned. But she waved at him and moved on.

There were plenty of fruit trees in the paddock, so Tess made her breakfast of apples and pears. She knew that year round she would be able to pick berries if she wanted them, and somewhere along the way there was a fast moving creek that she could get her drink from and clean up. But right now she just wanted her solitude.

Avalone was the Keep of Avalone Castle, The Fates' part of the realm. Their castle was not as large as Mel's, nor were the grounds as grand, but it was beautiful. On this land sat the Tree of Seasons, the tree of Magick. The tree had at one time been a part of Molavonta, the castle that the queen actually resided at, but there had been a problem with the waterways and it had been moved. Most people did not realize that it had ever been anywhere but where it sat now.

The sun was high in the sky when she walked into the first cave. It had been cleaned, she noticed, and someone had planted flowers along the outer rims of the entrance. She would have to tell her grandmother when she next visited her fairy ring where she had faded to when Tess's grandpa was murdered.

She had just gone past the first three mile mark below the surface when she heard the voices. She had not realized that anyone was here and nearly turned to leave them to their solitude. But something about what they were saying caught her attention and made her blood freeze in her veins.

"What do you mean there's a problem with the law? You're the one who told me it was perfect. That all I had to do was bring her before the Council of Magick and they would agree with me."

Tess did not know this voice, but she shuddered when the second man spoke.

"It is perfect, that's not the law I was referring to. It's the one about her childless state and that she should be able to have more than one as a queen. She had asked that it be put on the books for consideration a few years ago. She had wanted the law changed, stating that she may have more children if she wishes. I had tried stalling her and, as she doesn't have a mate, she hasn't tried pushing it forward anymore. But she may point that out at the trial. And it may come back that I have not done my duty to get it passed."

Councilman Trundle was plotting against the queen, it seemed. Tess wanted to turn away. The last time she had known about a plot against the queen Tess had been stripped of her rank and her family had been killed. But whether it was some misguided sense of duty or just being nosey, she stayed to listen.

"You just keep it on the books too. I don't want any more brats running around. Christ, those snotty little beings make me sick to my stomach. Besides, she won't be around long enough to breed anyway. Once we are truly wed and I have her bedded, I plan to take her immortality and kill her anyway. Queen Mel will just have to die. I don't have time to molly-coddle a stupid woman. I have a realm to run and a world to conquer. And unlike her first mate was able to do, I plan to kill her immediately while she lay sated in my bed."

"Yes, well you may want to take care of that bitch cousin of hers too before you do that. Sara has a mate that carries a great deal of weight with the Vampire Council. Aaron MacManus is not one to fuck with. I've tried before; he is too much for one man or demon to deal with."

"You just leave that so-called Master MacManus to me. Marlus, underlord will not be waylaid in this. Understand, little man? It is in your best interest that I succeed. If I fail, you fail as well."

When the voices went silent after a bit Tess stayed where she was until she was very sure they were actually gone. Then she leaned unsteadily against the stone wall and tried to think what she should do now.

Tess no longer worked for the queen and had not for some time. While she felt no loyalty toward her, Tess still had a keen sense of responsibility. If Tess told the Fates then she knew that they would tell the queen. Tess did not see any way of getting out of a face-to-face with the queen, however, and that more than anything would keep her from talking.

Turning to go back the way she had come, the outing now ruined for her, she made her way to the mouth of the cave. Nathaniel was there waiting for her.

"I thought you'd be gone by now. Gone back to the human world, I mean. Don't you have friends there, a job?"

"You're here. I have a case to settle, but I need only to write my findings. With the death of Manchester, thanks to you, the case is closed unless he wasn't alone. Why did you leave our bed, Tess?"

"It's my bed and I wanted to clear my head—it's my only day off this week. You shouldn't really concern yourself with what I do and don't do. Didn't you tell me once before that you didn't need or want a mate? Well, I don't want one either and, no matter what the Fates have said, I won't be taking you." She started down the hill toward the orchard and he kept pace with her. She did not run, though she wanted to. So she walked as she normally did when she had nowhere to be and no one to report to for a change, a pace that ate up the ground fairly fast.

"Tess, we really need to talk about our bond. Because I drank from you, as my mate, I can no longer feed from anyone else but my maker and he is dead. I'll need to be where you are."

"I'm well aware of what I have to do to accommodate your needs, Nathaniel. Why don't I just meet you somewhere and you can feed from me when you're…you know, hungry? That way you can go on with your life and I can mine. That's the way you wanted it in the first place, isn't it? At least until Athropos blackmailed you. You could have saved yourself a lot of trouble if you had just not fed me the first go around."

She had not meant for it to come out so mean, but she could not keep the conversation she had overheard in the caves from popping up and distracting her.

"So you have no intentions of completing this bond between us, do you? I thought that once we were together you'd change your mind. I never thought you to be a coward, Tess. And what I said before was wrong of me. I, at least, am willing to admit that."

"You have no right to think anything of me; you don't know me any more than the Fates do. You're the one who wanted this bond, not me. I refuse to move my life around to suit you or the Fates. Now, do you need me to meet you somewhere to feed every day or not?" She knew she had gone too far the moment he looked down at her. She had told him it would not work. She had told him not to do it. His anger was rolling off him in heated waves and touched her skin like a torch.

"I'll contact you when I need you. When I find your friend, Albadar, I'll have him take me home and I'll also make sure he has my cell phone number so you can contact me. Since you keep a tight hold on your mind and enjoy keeping me out it's the only way I know you can reach me. I should probably have yours as well, unless you'd rather I just waited until you got around to contacting me when you think I should need you." He looked off into the distance and then back down at her. "Things could be so different between us, Tess, if you had only allowed it. If you need me…well, I'll be seeing you around."

He turned on his heel and left her standing there. She stared after him until he was out of sight then she simply dropped to the ground on her knees. Tilting back her head to look at the sky she let the momentum pull her back and she landed on her back in the grass. She hurt. Her chest felt as though it had been crushed and she had been the one doing it.

Tess watched the clouds without seeing them. Birds flew over her head in singles and in groups and she barely noticed. If asked, Tess would not have been able to tell anyone what she was feeling nor why the tears streamed down her cheeks. Closing her eyes, she fell into a dreamless sleep. It was the perfect way to make the sudden pain in her chest go away.

Sometime later a shadow crossed Tess and woke her up. She stared up at the stranger to these lands for a few minutes before it spoke softly, telepathically through Tess's mind.

"You're Tess Knight, are you not? The queen has sent me to locate you. She has been hoping for some time now to speak with you, Lady Knight, if you please."

Tess sat up slowly and wondered how the messenger mist had found her. Then decided that she did not care; it was here now and she needed to deal with it. If she did not, then it would follow her everywhere until it delivered the message and took one back to the sender.

The messenger did not have a form, but was literally a cloud of energy that only looked like mist. The messenger was from one of the sacred mountains in Molavonta that bordered one side of the castle. To form a messenger mist a person needed to have a pure heart and an opened mind. The messenger would serve only the magical creature that formed it and would do so until their maker died. This one was a beautiful shade of light pink, which made it about three thousand years old. The brighter the color, the younger they were. This one had probably been serving the queen since it had been formed by her.

"Tell your queen that she and I have said all we need to. And that I wish that she would leave me alone. I have moved on with my life and she should as well. And that I would die happy if she would just fuck off."

Tess felt the being looking down at her with disapproval. She was sure that if it had a face it would be staring with wide eyes and opened mouth. She guessed they did not get many people telling them no when the queen sent a request or she summoned them.

"I cannot say that to my mistress, Lady Knight! She will be most displeased when I tell her that you do not wish to speak to her. I cannot think that she would be overly happy if I tell her that as well."

Tess rose to her feet and the being backed up. Tess could not harm the creature, but if they touched for too long it could absorb a lot of energy from Tess. She would not die, but she would be very weak for some time.

"Just tell your mistress that I am not coming to speak to her and for her to leave me alone. She has nothing to say to me that I wish to hear and I don't want to hear her try." Moving a few feet away Tess bowed low before the messenger. "Goodbye now."

The messenger rose high in the sky in a long stream of pale pink then shot away toward the distant mountain tops.

~~~

Nathaniel sat at his desk for another hour before he pushed the print button on his computer. He watched as the printer spewed out the report and the photos from the robbery/crime
~~~

scene. The disc with the camera footage was still in his drive and he sat up slightly to pull it out and put it into the case.

The crime boys had taken all the footage from all the cameras in the bank job and pieced them together into a long, continuous video for the file. It followed the eight men into the bank and filmed as each one of them met their death one by one by Tess's hand. She had never hesitated, nor had she flinched from anything or anyone while she took out the men, not even when she had been shot. The only deaths that Tess had had nothing to do with where the bank manager and Manchester himself, just as she had said. Manchester had first killed Thomas then later turned the gun on himself. There was no sound on the tapes from the bank, but it was obvious that Manchester had been in a great deal of pain just before he had done it.

There was no doubt in Nathaniel's mind that Tess had cared nothing for herself. She did not care if she lived or died at any point in the entire rescue. And if her taking on the armed men had not proven it, then watching her crawl away from help just before the police stormed the bank told it all. She had not been trying to get to help, but rather get away from it.

"Tremont! You're wanted in the office, ASAP. Boss wants to see you."

Nathaniel looked up at the other agent, nodded once, and stood. But not before slipping the disc that he had taken out of his computer and slipping it into his pocket.

He had already taken care of the lab boys who had put it together. He had had them make another version of the information that did not include Tess's face. It had taken him nearly four hours of re-edits to get it just right, and in the end he was satisfied no one would ever know Tess Knight was even in the bank. Not even the customers she had rescued knew that a lone woman had saved them, having never seen Tess at all.

"Want to tell me what the hell this is supposed to mean?"

Nathaniel caught the file tossed at him by his superior as soon as he walked into the office. He closed the door and opened the file. Sitting down, Nathaniel looked over at Special Agent Donaldson and sighed. He had hoped to leave without having to do this, but apparently not.

"I believe you can read as well as I can. It's my resignation, effective immediately. I told you last month this was my final case. You can't possibly be surprised by this." He tossed the file back on the desk.

"I'm surprised by the fact that you can even spell resignation. Now tell me the real reason you're quitting. That says personal reasons. Can't be too personal if you won't tell your best friend."

"What makes you think…ah hell, Justin, I've met my mate and I want to be with her. But I have to convince her that she wants to be with me."

Justin was a human and his best friend, as he had said. They had met while they had worked a crime scene together one night and Justin had been shot. Nathaniel, knowing that the young man had a new family, could not let him die. He had done something he had done for very few people in all his thirteen hundred years; he had opened his vein for a stranger. Justin had remembered, something very few others have done. Nathaniel had thought about trying to adjust his memories again, but had decided that he liked the man knowing. It was nice to have someone else to talk to for a change.

"Yeah, I can see her point. You are sort of ugly and homely-looking. Could be that she has better taste than you think. I like the girl already…it is a girl, right? What sort of things have you tried, to convince her that she needs you?

Brow beat her? Pistol whip her? While those can be enjoyable pastimes under certain circumstances, they are not necessarily all that good when you want a woman to fall in love with you."

"Of course it's a girl, you moronic asshole. You make it sound like you think this is entirely my fault. How do you know that I wasn't my charming self and she is the one pistol whipping me?" Nathaniel asked with a bite of anger.

"'Cause I know you. You can be a bully when you need to be, you can sometimes be pushy when the occasion warrants it, but charming you are not. Let me guess, you told her this is the way it was going to be and you probably used the line, 'it'll be good, you'll see,' right?" Justin leaned back in his chair and it was everything Nathaniel could do not to knock him backwards.

"So? What's your point? It will be good if she would just do it my way." As soon as the words were out of his mouth he knew he had done just that. And by the look on his friend's face, he did as well.

"I'm thinking I'll accept this resignation and let you go. I'll miss you, but I think you need this woman in your life much more than you need this job. Find her, my friend, and tell her you're sorry. And then tell her that every hour of every day until she believes you or kills you. And then name your firstborn after me."

Nathaniel left knowing he needed to find Tess.

Chapter Eight

"Sire, there is a man here to see you. He said that he has some important news to tell you. He said that his name is Tribuin. Shall I show him in?" Duncan asked Aaron.

"Of course. Take him to the half room. I'll be down soon. Has Sara left yet to get the children?"

"Yes, sire, she has gone to get the little ones from school. I will bring in some refreshments. This man, he is vampire I believe, and has two men with him. Bodyguards, he called them."

~~~

"My lady, a demon imp has entered the home of MacManus. There are three of them and two more shadowed. The missus is not in residence, nor are the children. I believe them to be at the school. The other two people of the house are in the kitchen. What would you like for us to do?"

Tess tensed. She had sent three of her men to the MacManus household the next night after what she had heard in the cave. They were not to engage, but to watch at all times. Since there were a few day walkers in the house she had sent someone to watch any vehicle that left and to watch over the
~~~

lair during the day. It had taken three extra men to keep up with the family's comings and goings. She had also been informed that the vampire Tremont had left four days ago and had not returned since. She knew this was it and needed to act quickly if she were to save the master vampire.

"Gather twenty men. I want you to take five more men and, when I give the word, gather the mate and children and take them to the household quickly. I want another three to keep the ones that are usually in the kitchen safe and out of harm's way. Tell five of them to watch the perimeter. The rest will be with me. Shamus, good work."

"Oh, and the vampire is back. He just arrived as the demon did. What shall I do with him?"

Damn it, Nathaniel was back. Now what? she thought, then she realized that he would either be a help or not, but right now she did not have time to think about it.

"Take three more men—experienced men—with you. He is old and will have powers that younger men won't be able to combat. And Shamus, tell them not to harm him or they'll answer to me, understand?"

"Yes, mistress. I will send Albadar with him. He is off today, but I believe he will not be happy if he is not involved."

Tess thought that was an understatement, but let it go. She needed to know that Nathaniel was safe and she was not going to think about why that mattered so much to her. Not yet anyway, not when she had just realized that she needed him.

Tess went to her house and dressed in her armor. There may not be a need, the man could be a friend of the master's, but she was not taking any chances.

Tess was naked by the time she walked into her bedroom, having chucked all her clothes starting at the door. She walked to the hidden panel in the wall and pressed her hand against the wall to engage the sensory system. Once it slid forward she put her thumb on the small pin and watched as blood welled from the puncture. It would read her DNA and only open for her. All the men in the Knights had a safe such as this. It kept their weapons out of the hands of any children they may have in the household.

The panel opened with a small hiss and she stepped in and reached for her leathers. Pulling them up over her legs she marveled again at the fit that accompanied their uniforms. The pants were loose until they buttoned. Once the last one was in place they molded and formed to her skin, becoming a protective shield against most common blades. Next came the t-shirt made of the same form-fitting material. It also protected her skin from the harsh bite of the chainmaille when she pulled it over her head.

Most people thought the protective metal was out of style as well as cumbersome and heavy, but this maille had been given to her by her great-grandfather when she was accepted in the Brianal Guard. She had tried giving it back to him when she had been disgraced, but he had told her to keep it, that he knew that she would again wear it someday.

Each member of the Knights was given a sword made especially for them. Size and weight calibrated to their hand and stance. Balance was important when in a fight and she would not have a man killed because his blade was not suitable for him. Tess still carried the one that the queen had given her. She had learned to fight with it and it fit her hand like an extension to her arm. She secured this to her back and then pulled on her knee-high boots, lacing them tight against her legs and securing the extra weaponry into them. Within twenty minutes of hearing about the demon imp she was standing outside the mansion with her troop.

"I don't know what the vamp looks like so we cannot attack when we enter. Plus, if the imp belongs to who I think it does, we cannot harm him without just cause or we will start another war with his owner. No one is to do anything until I say so, got it?"

When they nodded their agreement they moved into the large room where five men were sitting.

Tess had thought that the imp would keep his identity hidden from the vamp, but she did not know he could make himself seem like another vamp. She had never met the master, so she was not sure which man he was. Now her earlier admonishment about waiting for an attack was warranted.

While no one in the room could see her or her men she could see each of them. Pointing to six of her men she had them surround the shadowed men and, when they were in position, she had them kill them. She would not have her men harmed trying to keep the ones she was trying to protect walk into unseen forces. The guards that the imp had brought with him that were visible were flanked by two each of her team. Now all she needed to do was pause, listen to the conversation, and wait for one of them to make their move.

"You will see that things cannot continue on the way they are. Some of the other vamps in this and other realms are going to rebel once they find out that she is breaking the law."

"Frankly, I think you're wrong. The queen is going to reign for centuries more and as far as supporting her, I will do that as long as she needs me."

Tess had just found her man she thought with a smile.

When the imp stood, Tess walked silently behind him. She needed to wait until he made a move to harm the master, but knew that she could not wait too long. The imp could kill the larger vamp in seconds if he had enough power. When he reached into his jacket pocket she wrapped her hand on the hilt of the sword at her back. The imp pulled out a small package, not much bigger than an index card, and she saw the magic flare seconds before he tossed it at the vampire. She was too late to stop it from hitting the vampire, but not too late for her to dispatch the imp back to his maker in pieces.

The only sound that was heard was the small vibration of the air being sliced open when she pulled the sword out of the scabbard and brought it around to the imp. Tess did not slow her movements, but brought the sword around full swing and back into its holder as she moved to cover the vampire with her body. She was fully materialized before she hit Aaron full force, knocking him back hard into the chair and pressing the silver net that Tribuin had tossed onto Aaron deeper into his skin. It was unfortunate, but necessary.

The imp stood for several seconds, his body not yet registering what she had done to it until the blood starting spurting from his jugular. As Tribuin reached up to grab at the fatal wound his head tilted back and fell from his shoulders. Blood shot from his severed neck, shooting high and wild around the room and along Tess's back. The leather and maille was no match for the acidity of his blood and burned through it into her skin. Blisters formed immediately and burst when they filled. It was a full ten seconds before Tribuin's body dropped and another five before he disappeared. Tess stepped back and stood very still.

Pain ripped through her, tears formed in her eyes, and she felt faint. She knew that if she fell, the vampire in front of her would be touched with the blood she had tried to make sure he was not burned from. The door crashing open behind her had her turning. The scream of pain was out before she could stop it. Nathaniel was just suddenly there.

The two men that Tribuin had brought with him stood. Her men killed them both and then moved toward Nathaniel. Knowing that she would regret it, she jerked the netting off of Aaron and turned to her men and growled.

Pain. Pain like she had never felt before rippled over her, in her, and all over her. She knew that she was in bad shape, but Nathaniel would be killed if she did not act quickly.

"Stop, Shamus. This one, he is mine. Don't harm him or I will kill you both. Samuel, go to the kitchen and see that the others are safe. The imp was not brave enough to come here with only these men. Daniel, I want you to go to Avalone; bring back the Fates. I won't...you'll need to tell them what's happened."

"My mate! My family, I need to go to them." Aaron tried to move, but the silver had cut into him deep and he was in pain. It did not stop him from trying.

"Your family is safe. As soon as I realized who you where, I had my men take them. The people in the kitchen, they are safe as well. Mrs. MacManus and the three children are there now. I did not have her brought here, as I was not sure if you wanted the children to see this. I'm sorry about the silver, but it was there before I could act. Will you be all right, sire?"

Tess felt rather than saw Nathaniel move up behind her. She had turned her back to Nathaniel to face the master and could not see him, but she could feel him. His anger was palatable. It touched her in ways the tainted blood did not. She was not afraid of him, but she was afraid of what she would see when she saw him.

"Don't! You can't touch me. It's poison. I need to...I have to wash it off before it's safe.

"Yes," the master finally answered. "Once I feed I would like an explanation of what has happened, but I believe you need to go with your mate. We will meet here in one hour. Nathaniel, take her to your lair and heal her, please."

"I cannot, sire. The Fates will be here..." Tess started to argue. She was not used to giving someone the reins over her, but she was falling fast now.

"I can handle the Fates for now. Go. And if I see either of you before the one hour, I will make the pain you are currently experiencing, young lady, seem like a paper cut. Do I make myself understood?"

She could not answer. Nathaniel had put his arms around her hips and pulled her close to him without touching her back. She wanted to lean into him, but knew that the blisters would be just as toxic as the blood that had caused them. Instead, she put her hands over his and nodded. With her next breath she was in his lair. He still had not spoken a word.

~~~

Nathaniel turned on the shower as he moved them toward the bathroom. He had been burned once by demon blood so he knew how to care for the wounds. But he had never seen anyone who had been burned this badly and still lived, much less was still be upright.

There was not much left of the maille on the back so, moving around to the front of Tess, he peeled it off her shoulders and over her chest. He knew that he was hurting her, but she did not say a word and stood as still as she could while he worked. There were places where the chain was burned into her tender skin and some where the blisters had formed over it. He looked at her for a moment before he spoke.

"I need to get this off of you before I can heal you or the chain will heal into your skin. If I work at it slowly it won't hurt as badly, but it will take a long time. If I do it quickly it will hurt like hell, but it will be over with. Which way do you prefer?"

He did not want to do it either way, if he was honest with himself. He would much prefer her not hurt at all, but he knew that if he left this to anyone else and she cried out or, worse, screamed he would probably kill them. No, he thought, he would kill them.
~~~

"The blisters, they'll…you'll get the pus on you. It'll burn you. Maybe…maybe you should just let it go. The Fates will be able to…oh, Nathaniel, it hurts so badly."

Her tears tore him up inside. His heart clenched tight and he knew that if the man who had done this to her was not already dead and beyond him he would go get him and kill him again and again. "I'm going to help you, Tess. I'm going to yank it off then put you in the shower. I'll heal you there. Please don't turn me down on this, baby. I need to make sure you are safe."

"No, I won't. I don't know…I don't think I'll be able to stand once you do this. I may pass out. Please be careful that you aren't hurt as well, all right?"

"I have you, sweetheart, and I'll be careful." Standing in front of her, he put both his hands on her cheeks and wiped away the tears then leaned down and kissed her gently on the lips. When she wrapped her arms around his waist he moved his hands to her shoulders where the maille was still laying. Opening his mouth over hers and feeling her respond he grabbed the chain, jerked it down her back and dropped it on the floor, gathering her as she fell forward unconscious.

Chapter Nine

Sara came tumbling into the room just as Nathaniel was carrying Tess to the shower. Sara fell to her knees before her mate, tears falling freely from her cheeks. Aaron reached out and touched her cheek. He had not moved from his position in the chair; the silver had cut him deep and only she would be able to help him.

"Could you all leave us for a few moments? I believe my mate needs some reassurances."

"Mistress said not to leave you until the Fates arrived. And we only answer to her. I'm sorry, sire, but that is the way it is."

Aaron looked up at the fae who had not yet put his sword away. His face was determined and fierce-looking. "I see. Do you think your mistress would want you to watch me make love to my mate and feed from her? Because that is exactly what I plan to do as soon as she comes close enough for me to pull her into my lap. As a vampire sex goes hand in hand with feeding and healing, but I'm sure you know that. I'm not going to wait for your mistress to return. I need this."

Aaron watched as the men looked at one another then headed toward the door. He grinned when he realized that they were really torn about which was the lesser evil, watching him have sex or their mistress' wrath. Aaron thought the woman must be one hell of a leader to have such loyal men.

"We will be right outside. We are doing this under protest, sire. If she asks you, you will tell her this, will you not?" Shamus said, and Aaron could have sworn he saw a hint of a smile playing on the fae's face.

"Yes, she will know that I forced your hand. Thank you, gentlemen. Oh, and if you hear screaming, do not open that door. My lady Sara tends to scream when she has her…when she is very happy. And I intend to thrill her hoarse."

The men moved faster out the door. Aaron hurt, but not enough to not find the humor in the situation. He sobered when he looked at Sara. "Ah, love, it could have been much worse. The silver is gone now and the blood did not touch me thanks to our savior. I will heal once I feed from you."

"Oh, Aaron, I was so terrified when those men materialized in front of us. They didn't say a word, but grabbed us right out of the van and brought us here. Mac of course thought it was a great adventure and Lizzy is, as we speak, flirting with one of them in the kitchen. Brent nearly went wild when the man grabbed him; he had to put the poor boy to sleep so he wouldn't hurt himself. They wouldn't tell us anything. He kept saying that you were with their mistress and you would not be hurt. Now look at you. You are hurt."

"Yes, hurt, but not dead. Had that acidy blood hit these open wounds it would have gotten into my bloodstream and killed me, immortal or not. That woman, the one you're looking for, Tess, saved me at great harm to herself. She could have let it hit me, but she threw herself in harm's way. I owe her a great deal. Come here, love, I need you desperately." Aaron pulled Sara into his lap, careful of his wounds, and kissed her. The kiss was meant to comfort her, but it turned needy quickly. He wanted to bury himself deep into her as he fed, healing both his wounds and his heart. He loved her more than he ever had anyone and needed her more.

"Feed first, and then I'm going to ride you until I really scream."

Aaron felt his cock harden more at the thought of her riding him and moved his mouth lower to her throat. Inhaling deeply, he savored her scent and rocked up as she straddled his lap, legs open over his groin. Licking a path down her vein he found her beating pulse with his tongue, lapped at it, and felt it speed up. Need for her surged into him, hot and heavy.

"Sara, take off your shirt. I want to feed from your lovely breasts, please, baby." She pulled her blouse open by simply jerking the buttons off in her haste. He groaned when he noticed the scrap of lace that covered her nipples, which were hard and straining toward him. Without moving the bra he licked at the brown hard point and then suckled it into his mouth. Wrapping her fingers into his hair, Sara pulled him closer to her and moaned.

As much as he wanted to free her for him, his need was overwhelming and he bit her through the lace. Blood, rich and hot, spurted into his demanding mouth. He pulled hard, drew a mouthful of it, and felt her essences begin to heal him. Pulling her hips forward, he began to move her over his cock as he suckled, rocking them both into a heated frenzy. Her arousal poured into him, her scent stronger because of it.

Letting go of her breast, he unsnapped the front closure. Her ample breast filled his hand and he licked the wound closed. Taking another swipe at the creamy flesh, he helped her stand and began pulling at her pants. He wanted her, to taste her, to bring her to climax right now.

Her pants were down around her knees when he buried his face between her thighs, her clit already swollen with need and peeking out of her nether lips just for him. He pulled the tiny nubbin into his mouth and nipped at it, then laved the tiny wound with his tongue. Spreading her wide with his hands, he ran his fingers up between her legs and slowly pushed two into her heat even as he ate at her. Moving to the edge of his chair, he moved onto the floor and turned her around so that she could sit down. As soon as her ass hit the cushion he pulled her forward and licked her in earnest, devouring her like she was his last meal. His fingers fucked her quickly now, in and out, stretching her for him. When she began to beg, wanting him to finish her, he reached down with his free hand and began to unbutton his pants and free his cock. It sprang forward and seemingly reached for her heat. Wrapping his hand around his shaft he began pumping himself, waiting and ready for her release so that he could enter her.

He knew that if he slammed into her at the beginning of her climax she would be tight and wet. And from experience he knew that she would peak again before he found his own release within her heat. When Sara stiffened then tightened around his fingers he knew that she was close, and when she bowed up and screamed out his name he pulled her off the chair and onto his cock, slamming hard into her. As she bowed back against the seat again, baring her throat, he brought her forward toward him and bit her just as she sank her own teeth into him. He roared his own release around her throat, his cum filling her the way her blood did him.

When she settled around him spent, he licked the tiny wound closed and held her to him for long moments before he laid them both on the floor. Not releasing her, he reached over himself, pulled the seat cushion off the chair, settled it under his head, and pulled her over his chest.

Aaron knew that he was completely healed; her blood was so powerful and strong that even now he could feel it racing through his blood stream.

"Aaron, the woman who saved you, who was she? You said she was the one we were looking for, how do you know? And how did she happen to be here and know about our safety?"

"She's Nathaniel's mate and the woman from the bank robbery. I don't know the rest. She was injured very badly saving me and I hope that Nathaniel can save her. She isn't an immortal and she could die from this."

Aaron moved slightly and Sara sat up. They both knew that the men outside the door had heard them, but were too comfortable with their love to care. As Sara started to dress again he thought of something else. "She told one of the men to gather the Fates and bring them here. Why not Mel? I mean, why the Fates of all beings?"

"I don't know. Do you think she works for them somehow?"

"Hummm, good question, and I intend to find out. Hurry, love, if you continue to dally getting dressed we will never leave this room. You have a luscious body and I can't seem to get enough of it."

When the couple opened the door there were six men standing there. None of them would look at Aaron or Sara, but when they moved down the hall toward the kitchen the armed men surrounded them in a tight ring.

"Do you think this is necessary? I mean, the vampire is dead and there seems to be no other threat in the house," Aaron asked when the men said nothing.

"It wasn't a vamp, sire, but an imp, a demon imp. My mistress will explain it to you. I…could we please know where that vamp took her? We would like to make sure she is all right. She could be really hurt and not do a damned thing about it until it's too late. Damned stubborn girl," Shamus said with concern and worry written all over his face.

"That vamp is her mate and I guarantee that she is in good hands. They still have twenty minutes before they are required to return to this floor. If we don't hear from them by then I'll tell you where they are. Deal?" Aaron put out his hand to the man who was so obviously the second in command of these men. The man did not hesitate, but took the proffered hand and shook it, grinning at Aaron.

~~~

Nathaniel took the sponge from the corner of the tub and filled it with liquid soap. As the water rinsed away most of the poison he moved her braid and began soaping up her shoulders with one hand as he held her with the other. The soap would clean the blood off as well as the seeping pus. The smell was horrendous and he was happy she was not awake to feel what it had done to her.

The chainmaille had saved her from most of the blood having been made of magical fibers like it was, but it had also torn at the tender skin when he had pulled it off her. The worst was along her shoulders and upper back, but there were some smaller wounds along the cheeks of her ass as well.

He needed to feed her, to get his healing blood into her, but he also needed to get the wounds free of anything that might absorb into her skin when he did.

She began to stir just as he was rinsing off the lather. When she looked up at him he nearly cried out with joy. She was smiling at him.

"You hurt your hands when you touched the silver. You should have worn protection. What am I going to do with you if you can't remember that? I don't have time to keep telling you to be careful all the time."
~~~

Her voice was heavy and he could imagine she was still in a great deal of pain. She was trying to comfort him even as she hurt and Nathaniel, at that moment, he fell in love with her.

Leaning down, he took her mouth beneath his. He had meant only a quick touch of his mouth against hers, but she was warm and alive and he deepened it slightly before pulling away, but not letting go. “I’ll keep that in mind the next time you have blisters on your back the size of my fist. And they’ll heal soon enough.”

He cupped her chin and kissed her again, slower this time and longer. When she brushed her tongue over his lips he groaned and opened for her. He swiped her tongue with his and cupped her head closer to him. He wanted her, but knew that this could be the turning point of their relationship and did not want to rush her, not this time.

“I need to heal you, Tess. I would prefer that we did it here so that I don’t get carried away and, if I did, I can push you out and turn on the cold water if I need to.”

“You can’t, not now anyway. I need to find the Fates. I need their permission first for you to heal me. They…I can’t let you be hurt anymore.”

Chapter Ten

Tess left him standing in the shower and walked into the bedroom. She had grabbed a towel, but could not manage to dry herself without pulling on the open wounds on her back. She heard the shower turn off and turned to look at Nathaniel.

"I need to borrow a shirt; may I use one of yours? The Fates are here now and I need to speak to them."

He did not say anything to her, but went to his suitcase at the bottom of the bed, took out a shirt, and tossed it at her. She grabbed for it and moaned when it caused her a sharp pain. He was still naked and hard. She wanted to go to him, to feel him, to have him take her, but knew that she could not.

Turning her back to him, she struggled with pulling the shirt on. After several minutes he took the shirt from her and held it open so that she could slip it on.

Her pants were soaked and her boots were probably ruined, but she knew that if she tried to take them off he would help. If he helped her she was not sure she could stop from touching him.

"The Fates are here and, if they allow it, I'll explain to you what they'll let me do. I know that you hate me right now and I can't blame you, but…"

"I don't hate you. Why would you even think that? I don't understand what's going on, but I do know that I don't hate you. I'm trying for understanding and to be there for you, but I also can feel your pain. You're my mate, Tess, and though you haven't bonded with me, I have with you."

Reaching up, she ran her finger along his cheek and, without a word, moved to the door and out of his room. She knew he was right behind her, but he did not touch her. Going to the kitchen, she took a deep breath and opened the door.

To say that pandemonium had broken out in the room would have been an understatement. There were more beings in the room than there was enough air for.

Along with Duncan and Penny, who were trying to assemble enough food for them, there were seven of her men, the Fates, Bradley Wolff, Sara, and Aaron. Tess was relieved to see that Mel had not been notified.

"She isn't healed. I gave you a direct order to heal her. Why have you disobeyed me?" Aaron stood and stepped toward Nathaniel.

Before she could move, her men did for her. Swords were drawn and Tess and Nathaniel were both surrounded by six men in a flash. Shamus stood behind Aaron with his blade at the vamp's throat. If Aaron so much as moved they would cut him in half.

"Aaron, I would suggest you step back. These men are loyal to her and will kill you before you have the chance to say…what is that word you use, Albadar?" Clotho asked the man who had just shimmered into the room.

"Give, my lady. The word is give. Master, what is your word? Shall I have Shamus kill this man?"

Tess stared at Aaron for a full minute before she answered. She was angry. This man had ordered that Nathaniel heal her. Was that the only reason he had offered?

"Tess? The man asked you a question. Answer him. Please."

Tess glared at Athropos then turned back to her men. "No. Stand down. Albadar, take as many men as you need and check the perimeter and make sure there are no more Shadows lurking about. Shamus, take three men and check the gates. Make sure that there are no devises that will blow later. The rest of you will take turns on the house; make sure no one comes within ten yards of the door without checking with someone in the house if they are welcome. You guys did a great job today. The men that you killed were demon Shadows and I thank you for your help. Go."

As the men dispersed to do her bidding, Tess started to feel dizzy and knew that she had very little time before she passed out again. Reaching out, she grabbed for the counter and got Nathaniel instead. He picked her up and held her on his lap.

"He needs to know what I am and why I can't let him heal me. Tell him what he needs to know. Everything, please?" Darkness finally claimed her.

~~~

Nathaniel had taken Tess to the upper floors to put her to bed. Duncan had helped him make her comfortable and, once she was settled, Duncan refused to leave. Nathaniel wanted to stay with her himself, but knew that he was needed downstairs. He leaned down, kissed her pale lips, and looked at Duncan.

"If she wakes I would appreciate it if you'd call me, Duncan. I need to be with her. She won't let me heal her, but I still need to be with her."
~~~

"Master Nathaniel, if she even breathes differently I will come to you posthaste. She is very special to me and this house. She saved my master from great harm as well as the mistress and the babes. I would endure much to keep her safe for you. Go, be assured that she will not come to harm as long as I am here. I was quite the boxer in my day."

Nathaniel tried not to laugh, but then realized that the man was joking with him and grinned. "Yes, I'm sure you were quite good at it too. Thank you, Duncan. I'll be back as soon as we are finished below."

Nathaniel walked into the large room and noticed that someone, probably Duncan, had cleaned up the room and removed the area rug that had been covered with blood and seepage from the carnage.

"She's resting. I've put her into a deeper sleep, but I don't think she will stay that way for long. She is a tad…stubborn, I guess you could say."

"That's a little like saying that I'm a little bit old. Have a seat, Nathaniel. We waited on you." Aaron gestured toward the sofa.

"I want to get back to her so, if you don't mind, I'd like to know why I can't heal her and what other information I need that she's given you permission to tell me."

"Tess is a Black Knight. And I'm aware that you have figured that part out, but what you don't know is that I own her. I took her life from her when she was pressed into service for me," Athropos told the room. "Had I not, she would be dead now. I gave her purpose and a job. She is only alive because the men and women that she commands demand her attention and keep her from thinking of anything but them. Tess has been fighting wars and winning them since the week after her family was taken from her."

"What does that have to do with my healing her? I healed her before and there were no problems, why now?"

"Because she was not aware and could not tell you no. I put that stipulation into her demands when we made our contract. So long as she is aware that someone may heal her she cannot accept. It is the way she wanted it. She chooses not to be a true immortal as well. If she is wounded and it is severe enough, she will die. That is why that first time I told you to bond with her I was so angry with you both. If she bonds with you then your connection, your blood flowing in her veins, will give her a chance at survival if she should become hurt."

"Why not tell me this from the beginning? Don't you think I would have tried harder if I had known I was the difference between her life and death?"

"Did you love her then, Nathaniel? Or did you merely not want her to die? She bound me to the same rules that she is bound to. I cannot tell anyone our agreement unless she agrees. Her telling me to tell you allowed me to tell you this and anything else you want to know."

Nathaniel looked around the room and his eyes fell upon Sara. She knew something as well, he realized.

"She is also the last of her kind, the last Knight, the last warrior fae. Once she dies, and she will if she does not take her immortality—her true immortality, as is her rite of passage—there will never be another warrior born within her race," Sara told him sadly.

Christ, he thought. Rubbing his hand over his face he wondered if he would ever figure out how to keep her safe. And realized that was not the problem. The problem was making her his.

"The vampire or whatever he was, the one that came here today to kill us, why me and why my family? And how did

Tess know to be here at the precise time that he was?" Aaron asked.

"He wasn't a vampire; he only wanted you to think he was. He was a demon imp, a slave to an underlord, a very strong underlord. I overheard a conversation recently when I was walking in the Caves of Avalone. There are others involved, but not all the players are apparent yet," Tess said as she came stumbling into the room. Nathaniel flashed to her side quickly and pulled her into his arms. He tried to be gentle with her wounds, but he could tell that he had hurt her. "As for your involvement, it's because of the legion of vamps you control and the amount of strength you gained when you became Lady Sara's mate. He meant to kill her, but in order to do so he needed to get rid of you first."

"I tried, my lord, but she threatened me with a very sharp knife if I did not allow her to get up. She is quite forceful when she wishes to be, is she not?" Duncan came in just behind Tess.

"Duncan, could you please get the young warrior a glass of juice and some light food? And see if you can find her a couple of pain killers. And don't look at me like that. You'll take them or I'll kick your ass. I'm pretty sure I have the hometown advantage here. And as you're as weak as a cat, I think you should shut up and do as I say," Sara blustered at Tess.

Nathaniel laughed, but when both women looked at him he coughed hard and turned away. He was fairly sure that they could hurt him and, even in her current condition, he was sure Tess could by herself.

"You are no longer my boss. I don't have to listen to you anymore. And you know as well as I do that I am not young. Do you want this information or not?" Tess asked.

"You are still as stubborn as you were when you worked with me. You are in obvious pain and I want to help you. I owe you so much that…that I'll never be able to repay you. You…you saved my mate, Tess. Without your intervention Aaron would be…he'd be dead."

No one said a word for several minutes. Emotions were running high. Sara got up, kneeled before Tess, took her hands into hers, and looked up at her.

"I'm sorrier than I can ever say to you about what happened that day fifteen years ago. I should have listened to you. If nothing else, I should have at least investigated what you said. I didn't and now so many lives have been affected by Sherman's evil. I want you to know that he is gone, swallowed by a tree and forced to live out his days around happiness and people, humans. He'll never to be a part of our lives again. Your family cannot be put to rest like you wish, their bodies were cremated, but I want you to know that Mel and I have taken care of their memories, and their names have been put into the Book of Fae. They will never be forgotten for their bravery and for their loyalty. You have been exonerated of all charges and, if you will, Mel will reinstate you to your former rank. I'm so sorry, Tess."

"Tess, will you see the queen now? Will you let her beg for your forgiveness?" Athropos asked her.

Nathaniel pulled Tess close. No matter what she said, he was taking her home, home to Avalone.

"Not yet, I think. As much as I'd like to get this over with, I believe there is more going on than we know about. You say that you heard an underlord talking. Would you recognize his voice, Tess, if you heard it again?" Clotho asked.

"I don't need to, his name was Marlus. Councilman Trundle is the one who told him that he would need to take care around that bitch of a cousin to the queen and that Sara's mate was too strong to mess with, that he had tried before and lost. Marlus said that he would take care of the vamp and Sara. That neither of you would be a problem for him."

"I guess he didn't count on you helping, Lady Tessa," Athropos said with a grin.

Chapter Eleven

Marlus was just going into his bedroom when a very loud thud sounded from the living room. He knew that whatever had come into his home was not a stranger. The wards that he kept on his home kept all that he did not know from being able to enter without permission. Cautiously, he moved back to the room he had just left.

Moving to just the doorjamb, he saw the body first. Reaching out mentally he realized that the body was actually a dead one and that no one else was in the room or the house. Stepping into the room he saw who it was and ran to Tribuin and fell upon him.

His head lay a few feet from him and Marlus pulled it closer, using his legs to scissor it toward him. Picking it up, Marlus tried to set it back on his friend's shoulder but could not. With tears coursing down his cheeks Marlus laid the body down and aligned the head so that it appeared to be still whole. Hugging the body close to him, he cried for his friend and one time lover.

They had been turned at the same time, nearly the same day, and had learned to fight or be killed together. Marlus had been a selfish bastard as a human, and being turned into a demon had not improved his way of life. But Tribuin had stuck with him and, at times, protected him from the others. Soon it was just the two of them; they had killed all the others in their fight to survive.

Tribuin did not have the ambitions to become an underlord, but Marlus did. In fact, it was Tribuin's idea for Marlus to try for the position. It took him centuries of killing those above and below him, until finally he had caught the eye of the master and had been appointed this realm. The two of them had celebrated for weeks, taking human women from topside and pulling them beneath the earth for their pleasures before killing them.

It was then that they had become lovers. Marlus had just finished with a woman when he looked over at Tribuin's cock, hard with need as he watched two women having oral sex with each other. Marlus had felt his own cock surge with renewed desire as he watched his friend stroke his cock, fisting it hard in his hand. When a stream of pearly cum dripped from the tip Marlus leapt forward and licked the creamy fluid clean.

Tribuin groaned, but did not stop him when Marlus leaned down and took him into his mouth. He had never tasted a man before and found the flavor and texture quite delicious and heady. Cupping his own cock in his hand, Marlus began deep throating the other man's cock. Suddenly he felt one of the women come up behind him and begin licking his ass, her tongue going deep into his tight hole. He felt his balls tighten and ready to come.

"Let her take you into her mouth. Let her suckle you like you are me. I want to watch as you come down her throat. Do it, Marlus, let her suck your cock."

The second woman moved between Marlus' legs as he sucked cock. His ass was being reamed by one woman; his cock was being swallowed by another. When he heard Tribuin groan he was surprised by the first spurt of hot cum when it hit the back of his throat. Marlus started pumping into the woman at his cock hard, fucking her mouth with quick, punching thrusts. He was close, and when the woman at his ass inserted her finger into his tight channel he roared his release, coming hard.

It was long moments before he could move. And a few minutes longer before he realized that he had killed the woman beneath him by choking her to death with his cock. The thought that he had been so powerful hardened his cock again and he turned to the woman behind him, shoving his cock deep into her mouth, surging over and over into her throat as she rolled his balls in her hand.

Marlus felt Tribuin move up behind him and felt when Tribuin's cock moved against his tight hole. Excitement had him lean forward over the human female and he spread his legs wide for the man behind him, giving him full access to do whatever he wanted. Marlus watched the woman struggle to breathe around him, but he did not stop, excitement pushing him on. The slam of the cock into his ass had him burrow deeper into the woman and come hard again. Even as she died he spurted into her, and when Tribuin rocked into him from behind again he pulled free of her mouth and quickly jerked off, coming with his friend as he filled his ass with his hot cum.

Even lying beside his dead body, Marlus was hard for his friend. They had murdered many people after that, men and women, taking their pleasure even as their victims died, and now his partner was gone.

Marlus reached up to touch the wound. He needed to know who had killed him. He would exact revenge for his friend. As soon as his fingers brushed against the cut he leapt away and up, his claws digging into the ceiling of the room as he hissed and bared his fangs at the dead man.

His mind screamed at him. There was no way. They were all dead. He had been told that they were all gone, the species wiped from the earth and magical realms. Warrior fae were dead.

He hung there from the ceiling and contemplated what this meant. A warrior fae could kill him, their magic and power only exceeded by his own master. Marlus moved slowly down the wall, his claws biting deep marks into the wood, gouging the plaster as he went. He needed to summon his ally, bring him to the house immediately and find out why he had lied to Marlus.

It was over an hour before he came, over an hour with which Marlus had had to suffer with his terror of the unknown. His mind had gone into overdrive thinking how this man, the warrior fae, had gotten past his senses. He attacked his co-conspirator as soon as he breached the door.

"You lied! You said that you had them killed. You told me that they no longer posed a threat to me and my plans. You promised me. If you did what you said you had then why do I have a body here? Why is my friend dead?" Marlus flew at the man, clawing and biting at him, tossing him about the room as though he weighed nothing. Had he not been immortal Marlus would have killed the man.

"Stop this now! I will not have you acting like a hysterical woman. I don't understand what you're talking about. Now I want you to sit down and tell me what you mean. Who is dead and what do you think I lied to you about?"

"You did lie!"

When the man drew back his hand to hit Marlus, he shut up. He knew that he needed this man, his ally, but he also knew that once he got what he wanted he was going to kill him.

When Albadar straightened his clothing and sat down across from him Marlus took a deep breath before he began. As soon as he left, Marlus thought, he was going to treat himself to some whore and fuck her to death in Tribuin's memory. It would calm him and he would be able to think. But right now he had to play nice.

"Tribuin is dead. His body came back to me an hour ago. Only a fae could have done that. Fae are the only beings that can send a demon back to its owner once they kill them. This particular fae was a warrior, a warrior fae."

"How? That's not possible. Tribuin was at the house today, at the MacManus' with the others. I was off so I couldn't be with them when the plan was set up. But I know all the people that were there. Unless…"

"Unless what? What do you know?"

"A vamp was there. One I've never seen before. He could be fae and is marking himself as a vamp to throw us off. Yeah, that could be it. His name…I think his name was Tremount or Tra something. I'll find out. Last time I saw him, he was with Tess."

"You find out. If he's the one that killed my Tribuin, I will hunt him down and make him suffer. No one takes what is mine."

~~~

Albadar left the demon lord's house seething. First, because he hated the man summoning him and, secondly, he had not been able to kill that pansy Tribuin himself.

He had wanted the beautiful imp, wanted him so badly that Albadar had approached him one night. It had not turned out well. Tribuin had told him that he belonged to one man and
~~~

one man only and that once Marlus was king, Tribuin would be his second, leaving Albadar in the third position.

Albadar had wanted to kill him then, but knew that only a few could kill an underlord's imp. So he bided his time and now he realized he had waited too long. Damn it, he thought.

Mentally rubbing his hands together Albadar thought about the rest of his plot as he walked across the field of Avalone. The plan was going the way he had hoped otherwise. The queen would be killed, Aaron and his meddling family would be destroyed, and he would be king—no matter what that fool thought was going to happen. And Tess, Tess would be his, his to torture and to play with. To make her pay.

The Fates had told him that he would be Master in Arms. It was his position not hers, that bitch. He thought about the day Athropos had come to tell him that they had found another, someone more qualified, someone more able.

"You are not up to what we are looking for in a leader, not now," Athropos told him.

"What do you mean, my lady? You told me last week that I was the one you needed to make the team work, the one who would see the future."

His heart was pounding hard in his chest. He worked to calm it. It would do him no good to have her know the amount of rage he carried within him.

"I know what I said, Albadar, but we have located another. She is more of what we had in mind. She is special, someone that has already had the training we need to make our warriors strong. I would like for you to work with her, help her to acclimate with the others we have. This will be a good thing for you. You can learn from her. She will be a great teacher for you."

A teacher for him, she had said. Who was she kidding? He had done nothing but carry Tess's ass every day for the past fifteen years and he was sick of it. His time was here and now.

Chapter Twelve

Tess watched the room as they bustled around. She wanted to get up, but the pain radiating from her back made her very aware of the need to stay still. Besides, she could feel Nathaniel's cock beneath her and could not think past how hard it was.

When he had walked out of the bathroom, hard and ready, she had wanted nothing more than to drop before him and take him into her mouth. She had not finished before, wanting to feel as he came down her throat. She shifted slightly, hoping to relieve a little of her need by pressing her legs together. Nathaniel's low growl made her stop and turn slightly to look at him.

He leaned to her ear and nipped hard at her lobe. "If you don't want me to throw you against this table and take you, you had better sit still."

Her body heated with need. She could not have stopped the moan spilling from her lips if her life had depended on it. When the room suddenly stopped and turned to them she knew that they had heard her.

"I should take her…maybe I should take Tess to the other room and heal her now that I have permission. I do have permission to heal her, do I not?" The sisters nodded as he stood up. "She is in a great deal of pain and there is no reason why she cannot be healed."

"Of course. Just go into the living room and we'll give you all the privacy you need. Just come back here when you are finished," Aaron said.

Tess knew by the look on his face the big vamp he knew why she had moaned and it had had nothing to do with the pain in her back. She glared at him even as Nathaniel helped her stand. She was going to hurt that man. She was not sure how or when, but hurting him had become a priority to her.

"You have my permission to heal her, Nathaniel Patrick. She will be able to drink your blood to heal now that I've given you both my permission. That is all you'll need to feed her," Athropos said before they left.

Tess followed Nathaniel into the big room with the fireplace and watched as he sat in one of the high, wing-backed chairs next to the empty grate. She was disappointed that he had not sat on the couch and then realized that it was probably safer for them both where he was. She wanted him in the worst way, but she still did not want to bond with him.

"Come here and sit on my lap. You can feed from my wrist this way and I won't be too tempted to make love to you like this."

When he patted his thighs all Tess could think about was his cock and sitting on it as he surged into her. The pain receded only to be replaced with an overwhelming need to be thoroughly fucked by this man. "I want you inside of me. Deep and hard, but you can't. We can't bond. You understand that, right?"

He stood then and walked to her. She thought he was leaving the room, but then she heard the lock click into place. Her heart rate tripled and it was suddenly hard to take a deep breath.

"Take off your clothes." His voice was hard. The command was difficult to ignore and she was not sure she wanted to.

Looking at his face she began unbuttoning the shirt she had only just put on. When it slipped from her shoulders and fell to the floor she stood before him in her leathers and boots. Moving her hands to the buttons, she pushed each one through the hole until the last slid free and her pants loosened enough where she could step out of them. She started to lean down to take off the boots too, but Nathaniel dropped to his knee and began working the snaps.

"I'm going to feed you first. I'm going to stand behind you and watch as you drink from my vein. When I can touch you I'm going to pull you against me and touch you, feel you, slide my fingers into you. After I bring you to peak, I'm going to bend you over that chair and I'm going to fuck you hard, entering you from behind and ramming my cock deep into your sweet juices."

Blood rushed to her pussy, making it swell with need and wetness. She had to hold onto his shoulder as he finished with the second boot or fall to the floor beside him. When he threw the boot over his shoulder she watched as he ran his hands between her thighs, leaned in, and buried his nose into her. Her moan ripped from her lungs and filled the silence of the room.

"Nathaniel, please. I can't wait. I need you now." Her voice made her wetter in its deepness; it was husky and breathy, just as she felt.

"Turn around and I'll feed you." She turned around and saw the large mirror over the mantel. From where they were standing she could see her entire body and Nathaniel's.

She watched mesmerized as he slowly stripped off his own clothes. She watched as he pushed each button through the hole as he worked his way down the shirt. He did not open it until the last button was free and then he slipped it off his shoulders to the floor. Next, his pants. The belt came off quickly once he had it unbuckled. He stripped it from the fabric and tossed it down with the shirt. She watched as he toed off his shoes, first one then the other. His hands stilled when he opened the button at the top of his pants, stilled for so long she looked at his face.

He had been watching her watch him. His fangs were dropped and his eyes were no longer blue, but a deep crimson, his need bringing out his beast.

"If I take these off I'm going to fuck you first. I need to feed you to heal you. If I don't it's going to hurt when I touch you."

"I don't care. I want you right now."

"I do too, Tess, and so will you if I take you like this. But so long as I have these pants on I'll be able to think beyond where my cock wants to be. Come here, Tess. Let me watch you feed from me. My cock is hard enough to break through concrete right now and I don't know how much longer I'm going to last."

She took a step back and pressed her ass to his groin. He groaned and she smiled. She wanted him to feel as needy as her.

Nathaniel raised his wrist to his mouth and bit open a vein for her. She watched as his blood started to trickle from him and her mouth watered for a taste of him. She had not bonded with him the other day and she had never fed from him when conscious. She wanted, no, she needed to feel his blood fill her.

When he brought it to her mouth she held him to her with both hands and sealed her mouth over the wound. Ecstasy. He was hot and spicy; his blood was old and powerful and she could feel it surge into her veins. The wounds at her back healed and repaired with it.

Drawing deep on his wrist a second time, she felt him press his chest to her skin. Moaning, she closed her eyes, the sensation of his touching her and filling her suddenly too much. When his hand cupped her breast she nearly melted to the floor, and when he pinched her nipple she rubbed her ass against his cock again.

"Baby, if you keep this up I'm not going to last, I swear it. I'm only holding on by a thin thread as it is."

"Fuck me, please, Nathaniel, fuck me." She had pulled away from his wrist and he sealed the tiny puncture with his tongue as he leaned her over the chair.

He opened his pants quickly, jerked them down to his thighs, and plunged into her at the same time. Tess came, her body primed because of his words, his touch, and his cock.

He stilled behind her and she looked at his reflection in the mirror. He opened his eyes and grinned at her. "I'm afraid I'm going to move and come at the same time. I can't seem to help myself when I'm near you; I have to come inside of you."

"Don't stop, please. If you come inside me, you'll bring me too. Nathaniel, I want to feel you fill me with your cum. I want to feel your hot juices fill my pussy and run down my legs. Do it, fuck me."

Grabbing her hips hard, he pulled out to the tip of his cock and slammed into her. The pain/pleasure of his hard cock filling her had Tess ready to tumble again. When he repeated the move she cried out his name, leaned back against his chest, and bared her neck. His cock jerked again and she felt him spurt into her even as his teeth sank into her throat. Nathaniel slid his fingers into her wet pussy and pinched her clit and she came for the third time as he continued to pump into her with tight, hard jerks.

They stood that way for long moments as he fed from her. His body continued to surge into her even as her own body trembled and shook. When he pulled away finally, after sealing the wound at her neck, he fell back into the wingback.

"Christ, woman, you'll be the death of me yet. I've never in all my long years been so drained and energized as I am with you after sex. If we ever manage to make love slowly I'll probably expire from it."

She grinned at him. She supposed she should be angry that he had brought up other women after what they had just shared, but she believed what he had said and felt happy he had told her.

"We should get back. There is a lot to tell about all this and I'm sure there are plenty of questions too."

The trek back to the kitchen was made longer because they kept stopping to touch one another, kiss deeply, and taste any exposed skin.

Tess walked in first, Nathaniel needing a moment to bring his hard body back under some kind of control. She could not help but blush when they all turned and smiled at her, and she knew in that moment they knew what they had done in the other room. Raising her chin, she glared at each of them. It was Aaron's laughter that burst through her haze of embarrassment.

"Ah, Tess, you are both a job to be around and a joy. Come, tell us what you know and Duncan has made you some dinner. I would imagine that you are quite hungry after that…healing that took place."

Tess glared again and then Sara slapped him. Tess barely caught it, but she would swear the woman threatened her mate with no cheeseburger for a month if he did not behave. As far as Tess knew, vampires did not eat human food.

Nathaniel came in just as Duncan was setting a large platter of food in front of her. Nathaniel winked and sat in the chair next to her.

"Lady Tess, Penny made you a variety of foods. We did not know what one such as yourself would eat so she made a little of everything for you." And that is what it looked like too.

There were two huge slices of ham that had been fried and what looked to be four scrambled eggs, a rasher of bacon, fried potatoes with green peppers and onions, sliced fresh tomatoes, and several biscuits that were still warm from the oven. He set a large glass of milk and an equally large glass of orange juice beside the plate.

"Thanks, Dunc, but you shouldn't have gone to all this trouble." He looked so crestfallen that she nearly leapt up to hug him. "But if you have any more eggs, I sure could use a couple more. I do pack quite an appetite when I heal."

She glanced over at Aaron and his nod of approval made her feel something. She had never had many friends, but knew in that moment she had one for life. Without saying another word, she tucked into her food.

When Penny had the other four eggs ready and Duncan served them, Tess had already polished off nearly all the food. All that was left were two of the biscuits and half of one ham slice. When he set the eggs down she opened the bread, slid the eggs and ham onto them, and ate them as a sandwich. She looked up into his astonished face.

"If I lived here with you guys, I'd never fit in my armor, much less be able to move. This was the best dinner I've had in centuries. Thank you guys, so much."

"You are quite welcome, Lady Tess. My goodness, how does one afford to feed you? Miss Athropos said that you command several hundred men. Do they all eat as much as you do?"

"Yeah, but they'd eat more if they had something like this set before them. I'm not kidding, Dunc, Miss Penny, I may pay a visit to you two just to get a great meal like this. Thanks."

"You are welcome anytime, my lady. We would need at least a day to prepare for your visit. Just to lie in some supplies first, I believe."

The room burst with laughter. Duncan, however, looked slightly confused then went about refilling her milk and juice glasses.

"When you were in the caves did you see anyone else about? The reason I ask is I was wondering about what you said about it being promised to him," Aaron asked.

They had all moved around the kitchen and were now sitting in some of the chairs pulled from the table. Sara sat on Aaron's lap and Tess had been moved to Nathaniel's when she had finished eating. She liked it there, maybe a little too much.

"No. And I wondered about that as well. There aren't many beings that are welcome to Avalone, so whoever told them about the caves has to know the area well. Where I met up with them was not a place to come and go easily."

No one said anything for a full minute until Sara cleared her throat. Tess had not wanted to say it out loud, but they all knew what was going on.

"You think someone from your men is a part of this then, don't you? Probably one of the men who were here today in this house, isn't it?"

"Yes. I do believe so, but I don't know who. You were never in danger from him; I never separated my men so that any one of them was alone with any member of this household. I believe that whoever is in on it needs to remain hidden until they attack your queen."

"Mel needs to be made aware of this as soon as possible. Her life may already be in danger again even as we speak." Sara stood, but was stopped by Athropos.

"Wait, Sara. There's more, isn't there? Tell us, Tess," Athropos said as Sara sat back down.

Tess stood up and began pacing the room. Several times she stopped, but then continued in her walk. She was thinking and needed to work it out before she spoke.

"I think I need to go back to the bailey to work on the files. I don't know why, but I think that there is something there that I need to look at. If we could table this until tomorrow night then I'll have more information for you."

Tess took Nathaniel's hand and led him from the room. She needed to speak to him and when he got mad she did not want anyone else to hear it.

"You have to stay here. Wait before you get angry. I can't think when you're close, for one thing, and I need to get this figured out. You make me crazy with need and I can't think when you touch me. I can't be close to you without you touching me. See, no work will get done."

He grinned at her and she wanted to kiss him until he wanted her again. Leaning forward, she groaned. His cock was hard and pressed against her belly, needy and filled.

"See what I mean? I want you to stay here and watch the house. You'll know better than anyone what to watch for, including my men. I have already contacted Robert and he knows that you are to be in constant contact with him. He is out on the perimeter now, but will be in shortly to speak to you. And, Nathaniel, I don't know why yet, but I want you to pretend that Albadar is in your confidence. Something flashed in his mind today, hatred so strongly that he may have killed Aaron without a second's hesitation. Something isn't right."

"All right. But you'll keep someone with you at all times, correct? Take Shamus back with you."

She had already given Shamus the evening off, but nodded to Nathaniel. He would not know that once in the bailey, she was protected with magic.

When he leaned down to take her mouth, she opened under him. Oh to spend an eternity with this, she thought, and leaned into his body. He pushed her away gently and she smiled and left the mansion. She just hoped she could continue to see him without bonding with him. It was much too dangerous for him if she did.

Chapter Thirteen

"Aaron MacManus, please wake up. I've need of answers that only you can help me with."

Aaron rolled to his back. He could not feel the person or being in the room, but he had heard their voice.

"Damn it. I don't have all day. Wake your lazy ass up! Hurry about it too." Yeah, that voice was familiar.

"Tess? What the hell are you doing bothering me? Is something wrong with my mate? Are my children all right? There had better be a damned good reason…what the hell are you doing in my chamber?"

"Of course they're all right. And why wouldn't they be? I do have my best men on the job. I need some answers. Are you awake enough to listen and answer them yet?"

"You know no one is supposed to be able to enter this chamber once I seal the door. But you aren't really here, are you? I see. Someone once before entered this way. I wasn't very happy with her either. I wonder if she taught you this trick just to irritate me."

"No, I taught her. I'm older than Mel—you as well, for that matter. I'm here to ask you some questions, not the other way around. Will you? Answer them, I mean?"

Aaron looked at the shadow of the woman in front of him. He sat up a little higher in his bed then leaned against the massive headboard and regarded her.

Tess was older than Mel. That bore some thought and he wondered just how much older, then realized that it would not matter right now, if ever.

"If you went back to sleep I'll have you know I can and will hurt you in this form. I'm very strong and I need your help."

"I'm not asleep, Tess, but I am curious. How about a deal? A question and answer trade. I'll answer one of yours and you answer one of mine." He thought she would balk at the idea, but she surprised him once again.

"Done! Tell me what it means to pledge alliance to someone, a master?"

Shocked, he asked, "Why do you want to know?"

The ritual between a master and his subjects was sacred. He and others like him guarded their secrets with their lives.

"Is that your question to me, vamp? Because it seems like a waste of both our time, but I'll answer it if it is." Tess stopped pacing long enough to look at him.

"No, it is not." She was sharp as well as smart, he thought with a grin. "A person, and in my case, a master, would ask the subjects in his realm or territory to give a gift of their blood. The vamp pledges to me that he will keep our secrets, follow the laws of our kind, and keep peace. During times of great need he or she would come to my aide, no questions asked. In return I pledge to them that I will ensure their safety and protect them against others. I will also keep the laws and mete out punishment as the situation warrants it." Aaron watched

Tess pace. Wherever she was, he hoped that there was no rug beneath her feet or it would be worn through before evening.

"Please ask me your question. I burn with a need to ask more of you."

Aaron grinned. If she was not the most tenacious person he had ever met, he did not remember who it could have been. "Go ahead with another question, Tess. I'll keep track. You can trust me." He watched as she studied him for a moment or two.

"I had heard that. It is said that you are a man of honor and integrity. That your word, once given, is your bond, that your friendship is tight and that you are an easy man to laugh, and easier still to forgive."

"Thank you. That's the nicest thing I've heard in a while." He flushed with embarrassment. But her next words had him nearly laugh out loud. Nearly. She was much too prickly to tease just yet.

"I didn't say I believed it. I just said that it's been said about you. Sheesh. You take their blood during this pledging thingy. Why? And how much?"

Aaron was getting into areas where he would be giving up something his kind did not share. But she had saved his life and that of his family. He knew that she was asking to work something out and he wanted to help her.

"Tess, what you ask of me is something few other beings know. I'll answer your questions, but I believe I will be owed something more—something of value to you." At her nod, he continued. "As for the blood, very little actually, only a drop is needed. The blood is a gift of trust. I take their blood that is freely given as a sign of trust. I trust that I will never have to use the blood bond to find them or to…punish them, I guess you could call it. I can also use it to see what they are thinking without them being able to block me out. You have someone you think you need to not trust, don't you? Is this the person we spoke of today? Are you that much closer to figuring out who it is that has betrayed you?" He had not lived over fourteen hundred years and not gained some understanding of beings.

"I'm not sure. I've some better ideas of the who, but not quite sure of the why yet. And for some reason, I think that is the reason for the whole thing, including the bombing of my family. Okay? I'm a warrior and a fae, do you think this process is meant to work on me and my men like it does for you? To find them on battlegrounds or in times of need?"

She did not answer him directly, but he was not worried. Aaron knew she would eventually get to her reasons. "I honestly don't know. But as a warrior fae, you would be a master among fae, right?"

"I'm not really a warrior fae anymore. What I mean is, I'm a warrior and a fae, but not together. Athropos holds the parts that make me whole."

He knew that he looked confused. He was. She looked whole to him. He had heard of her abilities. What was she not whole with? he wondered. "She said you were bound to her. What does that mean? And I ask because it could be the answer to your own question."

She paced some more. Back and forth until Aaron was ready to say "give" just to have her stop.

"Athropos holds a part of both of me—the warrior and the fae. When my family was murdered, I…I went a little insane. I had decided to join them. My great-grandmother and grandmother had taken it very hard and asked to be put to the fade. But my mother took her own life. See, when their mates were stripped of their honor when they failed to protect the queen, they too became mortal. Just as I did the weeks before when Melody stripped mine when I tried to make her see reason. I was…you might say that I was a tad too forceful in my argument. I held her down at blade point and made her listen to me. It did me little good as you know, but I went against the queen regardless. My family would have been able to live for centuries more, but we could also be killed by any manner of human hurts. I went to the Fates…actually, I went on a rampage to get to the Fates and tried to kill them. I knew deep down that I couldn't, but I don't think at the time that was the point. Instead, I ran into a friend. Roger let me work off some of my anger and then he took me before them, the Fates. Athropos said she would give me what I wanted in exchange for parts of me. Without thinking, I agreed. She took one feather for my fae and my blood for my warrior. She alone can command me, and she alone can release me."

"A feather? Are you saying you have wings, Tess? That you fly? Christ, you must be magnificent!"

"Had wings. She holds the one that completes me. Focus here, fang face; I'm the one with the questions. With their blood, will I command them or merely know them?"

Laughing, he answered her. "With your strength, age, and power I would say both. Just how old are you anyway? And do you wish to go against Athropos and the Fates?"

She paced again, and this time it did not bother him. She was a thinker and one who rarely spoke without weighting each word she used. So he waited for her to work it out.

"I am one of the original Guard. I am nearly ten thousand years old. And I have seen more and done more than you will in many a lifetime, Aaron." He was shocked by her answer and how uncaring she was about it. "No, I don't plan to go against the Fates, and I couldn't anyway. As I've said, they own me. But I also cannot allow what is more than likely brewing to go without trying to stop it. There are things going on, things I can't figure out. I'm not one to be ill prepared. Which brings me to my final question."

Aaron was sure he was not going to like this one, knew it deep within his heart and soul. "Before you ask, I have one more for you, please? Your bond with Nathaniel, why won't you complete it for him, become his mate? What holds you back? Is it this thing that you think is going on? He could be a help more than you may realize."

"Why is it important that I complete it, to you I mean? He will change, as will I. Don't you believe that it is my duty as my mate to keep him safe, out of harm's way? He will take on my powers, as you call them, and I his. What would he lose? What will he gain? Those are questions you should be concerned with. I can't harm him, as fae and as his mate—harm none. We are taught that from infancy. "

"Yes, I believe the same thing. But completing the bond will make you one. You'll complete him, be his match in all things. That's it, isn't it? Bonding with him may make him mortal too. You're not completing it to save him from certain death."

"You know, for a young vampire you're not so dumb—at least not as dumb as I first thought. He must remain immortal. I won't be able to protect him and fight this coming war if I know he can be killed. We both know that no matter what I do or what I say he'll join the fight without thought to himself. I must take measures to ensure his safety above all else, even if it means never creating what I know will be the greatest thing in both our realms."

Aaron decided to ignore the comment on his intelligence and let her ask her final question. He really wished that he had not when she did.

"If I call upon you and your kind would you fight beside me or die because of me?"

~~~

Tess sat looking at the files of the men and women who fought with her. They lay spread out all over the desk and a few had scattered to the floor.

Each file had a drop of blood of the file's owner to signify their allegiance to her. Not to the Fates as she had been told, but to her personally. Why? she wondered. She got up and paced again.

Pacing had become a habit when she was learning to fight. It had not been so much pacing as it had been a way to be able to march long distances. She needed to keep up with the miles they would be required to go every day and she walked to keep in shape. When she had learned to use her wings to carry her over long distances the pacing had been a way to make sure she kept in the best possible shape she could. With it came the ability to clear her mind and think things out.

They were all fae, every man and woman who fought with her and beside her were of her kind save one, and that had to be significant too, but she could not see how just yet. Albadar was unknown to her as a species and, according to his file, he did not know what he was either. For some reason she did not believe him or the file.

The blood and the contract that accompanied it would be enough to bond them to her according to the vamp—if it was even possible. She believed now that it was. But what would the bond give them and her? What sort of hold, if any, would she have over them? Would they all become mortals as she was? She didn't think so. There was a reason, but she could not figure it out.

Sitting at the oversized desk she scanned the room to calm her mind. Shelves on one wall held books, some as old as time, others as new as yesterday. The types of books varied as well—books about legends and myths going back to the
~~~

beginning of magick, to the paperback romances that Shamus enjoyed. The next wall—and the only one that was nothing but a wall—held battlement and armor that she and her family had collected and used over the centuries. Some of them still carried the marks of war, others blades still honed to razor sharpness. Again, the varied amounts and styles were staggering—knives, helmets chainmaille and even boots—each from different centuries and different realms. The third wall was a bank of windows and mirrors, some tall some short. Others still were covered with parchment or heavy tapestry while most remained clear and open. They were the Windows of Time. No one used them much anymore, but they could be used to step back in time or into the future. Dragons used them to bend time, alter events, and delete or destroy times when there was too much happening and humans could not cope.

The wall behind her and the desk was filled with photos. Most of them paintings, some of simple drawings and sketches, but they were all of past fae warriors. Tess's family hung there with a black band across their hearts, the only warrior fae that had ever been killed.

When she felt calm enough and in control she picked up the second file in the stack closest to her and opened it. Shamus. He was the only person she had ever called friend, and the only man who had ever stood beside her in battle even after all the problems with the queen.

Making sure she still felt calm, she opened the file. She did worry that if she wasn't able to ease into this gently she might go pinging off his skull and harm him in some way—if she was able to enter his mind at all. Taking a deep breath she put the bloodied piece of parchment onto her tongue and waited.

Nothing happened. Just when she thought she had made a mistake in this whole theory, in tasting his blood and believing that it had something significant to do with her, she snapped into his head like a rubber band snapping onto skin.

It had been so long since she had walked a mind; she was clumsy at first and knew that he felt her when he kept looking over his shoulder for her. She gentled her search and felt him relax. That was when she realized he had looked over his shoulder and she could see what he did. She could see through his eyes and into whatever he was looking at.

Giddy now, she did what she had planned and called to him. Demanded really, and as much as she hated to do that it was the best plan she could think of right now to see what the powers would do.

"Shamus, I need you to come to me. I'm in the office of the bailey. Come now."

Within seconds he shimmered into the room, grinning and looking confused at the same time. "Well, if you don't look like the cat who ate the canary. What have you been doing?"

"Oh, Shamus, you have no idea. I need your help."

Chapter Fourteen

Aaron was sitting at the kitchen table when Nathaniel came up from his lair. He had been asked by Tess to watch the household and make sure that things were safe here. He knew that it was not busy work, there were several times when he had thought he had caught Albadar up to something, but the man had a good reason for being where he was at the time. Nathaniel still didn't like it. Something was up with the man and he just knew it.

"Your mate came to see me this afternoon. She just showed up in my chamber out of the blue," Aaron said in way of greeting.

Nathaniel felt his fangs lengthen and anger burned through his veins. Vampires did not meet with another's mate, no matter what. It was an unspoken rule that everyone knew and it would get you killed if you broke it. And here this man was seemingly bragging about it.

"She was only there in spirit, so you needn't worry that is was anything clandestine or anything. She had a few questions she needed me to answer. We had a deal, and I got a few answers from her as well. Would you like to know what we talked about?" Aaron shook his head as if thinking something over. "Well, I can tell you some; some of it I don't understand, but I'm sure it will come to light. How about it, Nathaniel? Would you like to find out a few things, like why she won't bond with you?"

"Are you trying to piss me off or are you seriously thinking I wouldn't want to know? She is, by and far, the most annoyingly stubborn woman I have ever met. But I think I've fallen in love with her. No, that's not true either; I have fallen in love with the stubborn little chit. Tell me something, have you ever met a woman you wanted to both strangle and make love to all at the same time? She makes me cross-eyed with anger and so needy for her that I find myself wanting to take her anywhere there is a hard surface." Nathaniel looked at the other vampire when he started laughing. Not just laughing, but holding ribs, leaning over trying to catch his breath laughing. He could only stare and amazement.

"Every day, my friend, every single day. But I will tell you this; there has never been a moment of boredom since I met my Sara. You will find that every day is an adventure and every night a walk into paradise. Sit down and I'll tell you everything I know."

Hours later, Nathaniel left the mansion and went to find a way to contact Athropos. He had a few questions of his own.

"Hello, Nathaniel Patrick Tremont. I understand you need my help. Before you ask me things, there is something you should know. I can only give you what you ask for, nothing more. You understand that, don't you? The bargain between Tess and myself is just that, between us. What can I do for you?" Athropos was saying as she shimmered into Blood Moon later that night.

The bar was for the supernatural, but lately it had been overrun by wannabes of all sorts of people, humans mostly, who wanted to be something they were not. He often wondered why humans wanted immortality. He himself had been around long enough to know that little changed in the larger scheme of things and what was there today would more than likely be back again someday. They did make a lot of money for the owners, one of which was Aaron, but it still caused problems with the humans and supes alike.

Nathaniel had a private room set up for the meeting with the Fate. He did not want to be overheard, nor did he want to have to beat off the patrons of the bar. Athropos was a very beautiful woman.

"No one has called me by my full name since I was a child, and it usually meant that I was either in a lot of trouble or my mother thought I was in a lot of trouble, which come to think of it, was correct in both cases. I hope in this time I'm neither. I've taken some notes on some information I have. And I have a few questions I'd like to see if you can answer for me. I want to know how you hold both halves of Tess and how does one get them back from you?"

Nathaniel had been a cop for many centuries in different capacities and he knew when someone was surprised by the information he had.

He watched as she pulled a charm bracelet from under her sleeve and showed it to him. "Do you know what a charm bracelet is? It's just that. A bracelet of charms, sometimes for specific things, others to have things or memories close to you. Sometimes it holds things. Like this one for instance, it holds the soul of a very powerful demon. We made a trade. He wanted me to do something and, in exchange, he gave me his soul. I get to keep it until such time that he can make a better bargain. Then I will give it back to him." She fingered a few more of the little pieces and then covered it back up with her sleeve. Athropos looked at him and smiled.

He knew he was missing something, but he needed a few minutes to figure it out. He also knew that she had told him the story for a reason, but surely it could not be that simple.

"I'd like to have my mate's fae and warrior parts, please.

"Of course. What do you have to trade for them?"

~~~

Nathaniel walked to just inside the office of the bailey and looked at the woman at the desk.

There were files and papers everywhere, the floor, desk, and a chair. There were even files lying atop the turned over trash can with a few odd things sitting there too. And Tess was asleep in the middle of all the mess.

He smiled when he heard her snore softly. Nathaniel realized then that he had never slept with her the entire night. They had had sex a few times, not near enough as far as he was concerned, but they had never slept together. He planned to fix that today.

When she stretched out and knocked a few files to the floor he leapt forward and grabbed for them. As he straightened up and looked at her she was standing and staring at him.

"How did you…you aren't supposed to be able to…you're not fae."

"No, I'm not. But you are and I wanted to see you. Athropos gave me permission to come here and to see you. It's up to you whether or not I can return, though. You look busy, is there something I can help you find?" He started walking toward her and tossed the files onto the mess on the desk.

"I don't—I was looking for something. I think I found it. There are files that I don't under…why are you here? I thought we had a deal, I come to you when you're ready to eat." She moved to the other side of the desk and kept pace with him,
~~~

but in the opposite direction. He did not care; he was on a mission.

"It's called feeding. I'm not sure why, but there you have it. I've come to talk to you, see if we can bond and become mates."

"No. I don't think that's a good idea. You have to leave, Nathaniel. I have work to do and you…you shouldn't be here."

He walked around to her side of the desk as she moved and grinned when she moved back away from him more. Nathaniel was not surprised by her move. What he was surprised by was her scent and her arousal. She wanted him as much as he did her.

"I found out some things about us, about you mostly. I had a long talk with Aaron too. He helped me understand a few things and then I got a lot more from Athropos."

"I'm going to stake that fucking vamp. He should learn to keep his mouth shut and his nose out of my business. Stop following me, will you? You're making me nervous."

"Then stop running from me. If you had come to me first, then it wouldn't have been necessary for him to interfere. We can bond, Tessa May. We can become one because we give our mates the best of us, not the other way around."

"What do you mean? Never mind, I don't care. I want you to leave right now. I have things to do and…you can't do this." Her voice had become husky and low. It sent shivers down his spine and though his bloodstream.

She had hit the wall that was full of battle gear. He wished she had hit one of the other walls, but he was glad she had had to stop. He didn't stop until he was close enough to feel her breath on his face.

"When you bond with me, love, I don't become mortal, which would be giving the worst of yourself to your mate. I give you my immortality because it's the best of the two of us.

You give me your powers of your fae heritage and I give you my vampirism that will make you stronger in addition to my immortality."

Nathaniel watched her face while she processed this. He could see that she was struggling with this new information and whether or not he may be telling her what he wanted her to believe. He didn't blame her for this. She loved him and she would want to keep him safe, just as she had told Aaron.

"I want to make love to you, Tess. I need you so badly that no matter how many times I try to relieve myself by jerking off I find myself wanting you more and more. The thought of drinking from you, sinking my fangs into your vein, makes me hard; the need to come inside of you makes my cock weep with need for you."

Before he could take his next breath she wrapped her arms around his neck and pulled him to her mouth.

Need and urgency pumped through her and into him. And when she opened her mouth under his he growled and pulled her closer, even as he pressed her to the wall.

Her dark leather pants were molded to her body, accentuating every curve of her, every muscle, and every feminine part. The vest she had on was sleeveless and cupping her breasts so tightly that her puckered nipples strained against the material. The lacing down the front hinted at the treasures he knew she had beneath, and he could not wait to sample her again. Her boots, darker than the other pair, had several buckles up the side and were cuffed at the knee. The soles were worn and looked to be as soft as butter.

Palming her breast, he rubbed his thumb over the peak and felt her shudder against him. She lifted her leg and he picked her up by lifting her ass up and pressing her against him so that she could wrap her legs around his hips. He rocked into her and she met him with a push of her own. He wasn't sure if he would last much longer and, as hard as he was, he suddenly did not care.

Nathaniel wrapped his hands around her pants, found the tab of her zipper in the back, and pulled it down. The pants immediately loosened in his hands, so much so that he could reach into them, cup her bare ass, and pull her against his cock. He would not have believed it possible, but he felt his cock harden and lengthen more.

“Drop your legs, baby, so I can get these off you. I’ve never seen anything…they were so tight. Now…now they’re not.”

“Magic. They mold to me so that when I fight they can protect me. I want you, Nathaniel, right now.”

Backing away from her slightly, he extended a claw from his finger tip and stripped the leather lacing from the grommets off her vest. He nearly whimpered when her breasts spilled out into his hands, filling them with her heat and their fullness. Lifting them in his hands, he leaned down, took the first hard nipple into his mouth, and suckled. She tasted like a piece of heaven and he needed more of her.

Dropping to his knees, he peeled the leathers from her hips and started kissing the exposed skin as he did. She was warm and soft, her skin was silky and muscled, her legs long and toned. Pulling the leathers completely off her, he sat back on his heels and looked at her body. He had had sex with her several times, but he realized this was the first time he had ever seen her fully naked. His cock ached with a need to be inside her.

With his hands on her hips he pulled her forward slightly and licked at the tight curls at the apex of her thighs. She bucked against him hard. Her clitoris peeked out from her nether lips and he nudged his tongue into her sheath and teased the little nubbin with his tongue and teeth. She cried out and wound her fingers tightly into his hair to hold him in place. He knew that he was not going to last long and wanted them to complete this now.

"I don't have a dagger to cut me with so you can take me. But I need to have you drink from me, Tess; I need to feel you sip from my body as my mate. Do you think you can bite me, drink from me?"

"I have fangs. I've always had them; it's a part of who I am. I'm not going to last, Nathaniel. I think the moment your cock is inside me, I'm going to come, and I'm so close."

Nathaniel stood quickly and took off his clothes. His cock jutted forward and wept with need. A stream of pre-cum glistened at the tip and hung from the end. When Tess reached forward and ran her thumb over him, gathering the cream, he nearly came when she put it into his mouth and suckled it clean. Her moan was like her fingers running along his shaft and grabbing his balls.

Picking her up, wrapping her legs around him, he dropped to his knees and brought the two of them together against the floor. His cock slid home as soon as her back touched the floor, her juices making the slide easy but no less tight. His balls drew up and against his body and he knew that one or two strokes into her and it would be over.

"Baby, you have to bite me when we come. I'm not going to last long, are you sure about this?"

"I don't…I've never bitten anyone before. I don't want to hurt you, but I need to taste you so badly. Please, tell me how to…Nathaniel, I'm going to come. I need to come, please."

Laying his forehead onto her he took several deep breaths. His heart was pounding and his cock was throbbing. Even the thought of her teeth sinking into him had him aching with a need like he had never felt before.

"You'll need to find my vein, the pulse. Run your tongue down the…Christ, baby, not yet. I'm going to come if you do that again. When you find the pounding pulse, bite there. Oh Tess, please…"

Her tongue was hot and wet and when he felt her teeth scrape along his jugular, he roared his release. When she sank her teeth into him and drew her first mouthful of him, he felt the room tilt and haze over, the corners of his vision closing in on him. Before he passed out from the overwhelming feelings and emotions she pulled from him with her bite he leaned forward and sank his teeth into her as well.

Chapter Fifteen

When Tess woke the next time, she was in her bed. Turing slightly, she looked at the man next to her. His face was turned upward and his long hair was mussed about his head. His grip on her waist was tight and snug. She moved a lock of hair away from his eyes and looked at him.

He was devastatingly handsome. From the deep vee of the widow's peak at his forehead to the bottom of his big feet and every part of him in between. And looking at his in-betweens, she felt her mouth water.

His cock was semi-flaccid, but still firm. She felt her body respond to the memory of him being inside of her and the taste of him when she had captured the cum on his cock. She wanted more of him, more than just a taste. She wanted all of him. Grinning, she moved slowly down the bed without waking him and wondered if he would enjoy this. Then she thought that she would, so he would just have to live with it.

Pulling her hair behind her head with one hand, she closed her mouth over the bulbous head of him and licked.

Rapture. That was the only way to describe how it felt to have him in her mouth, the taste of him, the texture and feel.

Wrapping her lips around him, she ran her tongue around his crown and then slid her mouth down the length of him as he hardened under her tongue. Shifting her hand down his cock, she used her saliva to ease her slide up and down him. When he groaned and surged up she looked up at him, saw that he was still sleeping, and moved her mind into his.

His thoughts were erotic and vivid. She and he were writhing on the bed, tasting each other and touching everywhere. Her pussy wept with need. She needed him to be inside her just as he was dreaming about. But she was enjoying this part of him too much to stop. He began to pump hard into her mouth and she felt his hand at her head. Looking up, she caught his glazed look. His eyes were red and his fangs dug deep into his lower lip. She could feel her juices trickle down her thighs, the thought of him and his cock making her body ready for him.

She thought he would make her stop, but he just watched her, pumping into her and moaning deep from his throat as she licking and sucked at him. Her hand began to pump harder and faster. She needed to press her legs together to try and give her clit what it wanted, the feel of something stroking it hard and fast.

"As much as I love what you're doing I want you to ride me, Tess. Take my cock into you and ride me until we come together. Please, baby. I can feel you're close, so close I can almost taste you on my tongue." His voice made her pussy clench and her clit hum with need. A tiny climax jerked her body and she rolled her eyes back at the sensations.

Taking one last lick across the tip, she crawled slowly up him and knew that he loved what he was seeing. Her breasts swayed with her hips and when she whirled her tongue in his navel he nearly came up off the bed in his need and pulled her over him. His mouth seared into hers; his tongue burned a path along her lips and then along her tongue as he fought and dueled with hers. She felt him adjust her and when he entered her, she threw back her head and screamed out his name when her peak caught her by surprise. When his mouth moved down the column of her throat she knew that he was going to bite her and she would come again. Nuzzling deep into the crook of his shoulder and neck, she found his pulse and bit him hard and quick just as he sank his sharp teeth into her jugular just below her ear. She came again even as his hot cum filled her, heated her, and claimed her.

~~~

They were in her office when Shamus came in. He took one look at Tess and winked at Nathaniel. "I see you finally got her to say yes. She is a tough nut to crack sometimes, but once you get her to open up she's not so bad."

"Hello! Sitting right here. And you have no room to talk, asshole. I don't see you taking a mate either. What happened to the last woman again? Oh yeah, she left you because you never spent any time with her. Bugger off or help. I was trying to explain to Nathaniel what I'm doing."

"She's trying to figure out what one of her own is up to, if anything at all. But as she is never wrong—just ask her and she'll tell you—I believe this time she just may be onto something," Shamus said to Nathaniel, then continued to Tess. "And as for a mate, I've found her, she just isn't aware of it yet. She needed time and I wasn't ready to make my move. But soon, very soon now."

"What is it you think this fae is up to and why?" Nathaniel watched as Tess got up to pace. He had noticed last night that she did that a lot. He was not going to complain. He especially liked watching her walk in the opposite direction from him. He was leaning over to look at her when he saw that Shamus was
~~~

grinning at him. Flushing, he sat back in his chair and glared at the fae.

"He's not fae. According to his file he is an unknown species, even to himself. I don't think that's true. If he was anything at all someone would have felt him, sort of recognized his as one of their own. I don't think that anyone could live as long as he has and not have a clue as to what species he is. I just don't think it's possible. Then there is the fact of his file. There are inconsistencies in it."

Nathaniel took the file she handed him and opened it to the first page. The first thing he noticed was the picture. The man looked…well, he looked evil. Nathaniel had worked with enough evil men to know one when he saw one. Then there was the tiny dot of blood in what he would call an evidence baggie. Looking over, he saw several other open files and none of them had the small bag with the blood in it. Nathaniel looked over at Shamus.

"She took mine first. To see what would happen. I was at a bar, The Otherworld, when she did it. I'm just glad I wasn't with a woman. She can see what they see, what I saw. Then she summoned me. I was compelled to come to her. Like immediately. Then when I got here, she had this shit-eating grin on her face and I just knew she had figured something…"

"You took another man's blood!" He had not meant to roar, but the thought of her drinking from another man sent him into overdrive.

Suddenly the room filled with soldiers. Their weapons were drawn and they were all pointed at him. Nathaniel did not move; he barely breathed as he looked over at Tess.

"They are more protective than before and quicker to come when they feel me being threatened. It's weird, it's like we have this lifeline connection. I can feel each of them as if they're a part of me, yet it isn't something that feels intrusive to them or me. It's all right, guys; he was just being a vampire. I'll take care of him. Thank you."

"You called them to come and get me?" Nathaniel asked as they left the room. He was not upset by them coming to her, but if she had called them, that was a different matter altogether.

"No, they could feel my anger, I guess, or something. At least that's what…shit! You don't think…Shamus, did you feel anything last night? I mean did you…you know, did you know that Nathaniel was with me?"

He sat there for a long time and Nathaniel thought he was going to have to kill the fae for upsetting his mate when Shamus looked up at her frowning.

"No. Funny, I thought for sure we would too. I mean, you can feel me by just thinking about me, but I can't do the same for you. I can feel you there, sort of in the background. Not that I was trying to see, it's just…wait, the Book of Knights. I saw something here." He hopped up and ran to the wall of books.

Nathaniel watched him sort through the stacks of books, pull a huge volume, and put it on the floor between them. When Tess sat on the floor in front of him Nathaniel slid out of his chair and cradled her in his lap.

"How many of the files did you take the blood from? There looks to be about three hundred of them," he asked as she settled against him.

"All of the leaders. And there are four hundred and ten of them, not counting Albadar or Shamus. I command over six thousand men. I didn't summon them all, just Shamus, but every few I would see if I could see what they were doing. I got better at it as the night wore on, but it is exhausting. Some of the younger men, I could see their thoughts, their…I don't know, their need to do what was right, but the older ones I got a stronger connection."

Nathaniel looked at her. She was a master now. He wondered if he could do the same through their connection. He was about to try and speak to Shamus when Tess moved her braid off her neck and bared her shoulders to him.

He found he could not keep from touching her, any part of her. While the fae turned pages Nathaniel ran his tongue along her bare shoulder. Her taste was intoxicating and delicious. And he wanted her again—here and now. He moved his cock up and into her as she sat on his lap. He ached with need to connect with her again, on the floor, the wall, the desk, chair—he didn't care where.

"I want you," he whispered through her mind even as he ran his tongue along her other shoulder.

"Okay, here it is. But I want you to stop what you're doing to her so I can look her in the eye. It says here that as long as the master and mate are within their own chambers—I'm assuming they mean house here and not just the bedroom—you will be closed to the others. So what you are currently doing to her, we can all feel it. If you keep it up you're not going to get a lick of work out of anyone for the rest of the day except for a bunch of sweaty bodies acting out your feelings. And I gotta tell you, Lady Tess, right now I want a woman so bad I hurt as much as your mate. I think my proximity doesn't help either. So cut it out."

Nathaniel chuckled when Tess stiffened in his arms. He personally could not see what the harm was for everyone to be as happy as he was right now, but Shamus was right, they needed to be more careful, especially when around a room full of others. Then he wondered if their connection would be felt with other species as well.

"Holy Crap! Tess, look at this. I think I found why the blood in is in the file."

~~~

Tess closed her eyes and leaned back against Nathaniel. A war, it said—a war that only she could prevent or every bit of magic would be gone.

Keeping her eyes closed she called to Athropos. She did not think the Fate would come, but within seconds she shimmered into the office.

"I see you two have been busy. Hello, Lord Shamus. Having fun with the underlings still? Nathaniel, you should know that you are now Lord of the Knights, that your command is second only to Tess's. The men will know this without being told. It's the deep connection you have with Tess. Shamus will be the second to Tess; you will need to find yours as well. He will show himself to you soon. I don't think I ever mentioned that to Tess before, the succession of the realm. Frankly, I never thought she'd be still long enough to find a mate, but there you have it. What is it I can do for you three?"

"I want you to tell me what Albadar is if you can. And I want to know if you know the outcome of this war. I'm sure you do, but I want you to tell me."

"What do you think? I'm Fate, Athropos, the cutter of the thread of life and I choose the manner of a person's death. I'm not the seer of the future. If you want answers, ask the question you really want to know, Tess, not the ones you already know the answers to. You are not stupid, nor are you slow. What is Albadar? What do you believe has the power to hide what they are better than any other species we know? What kind of power does he wield and where is he getting it from?"

She stood to pace. If Albadar was who she thought he was, then why was he working for her? Or was he? Was he
~~~

gathering information, or did he have a deeper reasoning behind this all? Why was he pretending to be an unknown and what were his plans? She stopped suddenly and looked at the Fate.

"He's a demon lord. The closest thing to the overlord there is. If he is here and pretending to work for me then he is up to something that he has been planning for a very long time. But what? I just know that Marlus has something to do with this. But how would two demon lords want the same thing in the same realm? Marlus was the lover of the man I killed at the MacManus mansion, so I know that he is involved somehow."

"Power? Is he looking for his own power or do the two men think to combine theirs to make a better stance? In the order of rank, what is the difference between the three levels of men?" Nathaniel asked as he sat back in the chair. She had gotten up and wished now that she had not. She wanted to be back in his arms. Actually, she wanted to be in bed with him and him over…

Shamus clearing his throat had her remembering that he could feel her emotions. Flushing, she looked at Nathaniel and saw his smile. This was going to take some getting used to, she thought with a frown.

"There are actually several levels, but the ones we need to work with are this— imp, what Tribuin was. He was elevated in his rank because he was the lover of the underlord, Marlus. Marlus as an underlord controls a realm or territory and the size would depend on what he has done to earn it. The bigger the bad ass in this case, the larger his territory, much like drug lords in your world. Marlus' territory isn't very large, but he needs only answer to the one above him, which is a lord. The only barron lord that I was aware of is William, but he isn't interested in expanding his realm. Then there is the lord. There are only a few dozen lords at that level; the one in this area is

Lord Tankin. Not too bad of a guy really if you get past the horns, long tail, and hell-like heat." Shamus opened the book to a drawing and turned the picture to Nathaniel. Tess looked at Athropos.

"Lord Tankin doesn't know about this. I'm sure of it. He is a fair man even for a demon and he owes me a favor," Tess said as she paced. She nearly missed the exchange of looks between the two men and she decided that she may have to hurt one or both of them for it. Men could be such asses.

"You said that he tried to claim the queen, right? He gave her fair warning, which is the only way he can take it from her without bringing down the wrath of Lord Tankin. If Lord Tankin knows about this, then why isn't he taking the kingdom from her himself? Unless…unless Marlus is planning to take the kingdom then wipe out his lord in the process. I still can't make the connection between Albadar and…shit! The trial of Council! That's why Councilman Trundle is involved. He gave Marlus the laws, gave him access to Avalone, and he is going to side with the underlord. When does Marlus try to claim the kingdom from the queen?"

Athropos smiled at her and answered. It was not good, not good at all. "Tomorrow morning at nine o'clock in the throne room. And Tess, you are going to need all the help you can get."

Chapter Sixteen

Calling the men together would have been impossible, but with her newfound power she called to each leader mentally and told them of her plan. She also let them know that her mate would be in command as well. Each leader told her of their happiness for her and told her they would fight for him as they did her.

"Everyone is needed to be in the great hall at seven tomorrow morning. Dressed for battle and armed for war. Any member who is with child or is to have a child born, male or female, will not be there. Any member with no children will not attend, do I make myself clear?"

"Yes, my lady, we will pass this on to the troops."

Satisfied, she looked at Shamus and Nathaniel. "He'll need to be armed and dressed. Can you take him to the armament and take care of this for me, Shamus?"

"Tess, I'm going with you. If you are going to see Aaron, I'm going with you. You'll need me and I will be going."

"As will I, my lady. This battle can only be fought and won if we work together. We all go."

She looked at the two men and realized that they would follow; even Shamus would disobey her and go if she left him here under the pretense of giving him other work. He would simply find someone to complete the task and then follow her. Tess nodded and held onto Nathaniel's hand. She looked at Athropos. "Will you allow him free passage? He is my mate and I claim him as such…I need him here," Tess told Athropos as she stared into Nathaniel's eyes.

"He has it already, my dear. The moment he opened your vein and drank from you. You only needed to accept him to allow him the ability to use the powers. Welcome to Avalone, Nathaniel Patrick, and welcome to our realm. Good luck with the vamp."

Tess shimmered into the MacManus kitchen seconds later. She was dressed not for war, but for a meeting of masters. She brought him a gift, a token of her faith in him as a leader. She was not surprised to see Sara there as well as Duncan and Miss Penny.

"I have for you a gift from a Master of the Black Knights to a master of this realm. I've come to ask for your help as leader among men and a leader of your kind. I've come to ask for your answer, master." Tess laid before him something that was very dear to her heart, her father's sword. "I give you this sword as a gift, not of my blood, but of my heart. I would be honored if you would use it to fight beside me with our men."

She held her breath as he stood. Tess knew that Aaron had fought during the centuries when swords were a way of life and not a decoration to hang upon the wall to admire. She knew the moment he took it out of the scabbard, the gold and bejeweled one her great-grandfather had made for his son, who had passed it on to his, would know how to use it. Aaron held it before him and looked down the sharp blade at her.

"You honor me, Lady Tessa Knight, Master of the Warrior Fae, with this gift. As a token of my faith and a gift of not my blood but my heart I give you my loyalty and this sword. I will fight not only beside of you, but in front of you and at your back. You have my men to rally with you during this time of need and to celebrate with you when we have defeated your enemy. I give you my word, my bond and my honor."

Tess looked at Sara. She was crying, pride showing on her face. She must have told Aaron what to say. He had repeated the bond of loyalty perfectly, and him now bringing the sword tip across his palm and holding it out to her sealed their contract as only a fae would know. She took out her own sword from her back, sliced her own palm open, and they clasped hands then hugged with the other hand at the back.

She sat down with him, overwrought with emotion, and told him of the plan and what she needed for him and his men to do.

~~~

After speaking to Aaron and gaining his help he suggested they go to Colin Larimore and ask the same of them. Both men were very powerful masters and brought with them more vampires than Tess had thought possible. She made sure that they gave their men the option of coming or not. She was responsible for her own men and did not want to lead men she didn't know to their possible deaths. If only half of their combined warriors showed up she would have nearly six thousand more men at her back.

After taking Nathaniel to the armory and suiting him up they went back to her home. She was exhausted and she thought he looked tired as well.

"We may die tomorrow. All those men and women may be following me to their deaths. What will I do if I'm wrong?"
~~~

"You know you're not, love. You may not be sure what is going to happen, but you know the players. Come to bed. I want to make love to you properly."

In their bedroom, because it could no longer be just hers, he kissed her softly on the mouth. He did not touch her anywhere else but her soft, warm lips. It was by far the most erotic thing she had ever felt.

She stood still as he undressed her. First taking off her shirt, slowly unbuttoning each button and leaving the shirt closed when he was finished. Going down on his knees he reached behind her and unzipped her leathers. The sound of it loud in the quiet of the room made her weak in the knees as he finished working down the mechanism. When they loosened on her hips he pulled them down over her thighs, and kissed her hips as the material moved along in a whisper along her skin.

"Nathaniel, please."

"No, not this time, love. I won't be hurried. I'm going to make love to you slowly and at my own pace. You'll thank me for it later—much, much later."

When he got the pant legs to her knees he licked the back of her knees and kissed the muscled calf of her legs, massaged her ankles. She couldn't help it, she moaned. Her legs felt shaky and weak.

Picking up her right foot he slid the leather over it then kissed her foot. Then taking her foot close to his mouth, she watched as he pulled one toe at a time into his mouth and suckled and nibbled lightly on it before moving to the next one. She would never have thought there was anything erotic about watching someone suck on her toes, but she nearly came when he picked up her other foot and did the same thing.

Standing before him in just her unbuttoned shirt and panties, she felt a trickle of her juices going down her leg. She was panting when he leaned forward and lapped at the wetness on her, she whimpered when he followed the trail back up to her clitoris hidden just beyond the scrap of material of her soaked panties.

"I'm going to eat you now. Drink your nectar and fuck you with my tongue until you can't stand up anymore."

"I can't stand now. Please, Nathaniel, take me to bed."

"Not yet. I'm going to drink from you here, Tess. I'm going to sip your juices from you and, when you come, I'm going to bite you and drink from you here. All right?"

She could barely manage to take a breath she was so needy, and her hissed yes was all he needed as he moved between her legs, ripping her panties away with a sharp tug. His tongue followed her slit from her gate to the tip of her clit. She shuddered when he suckled the hard nub into his mouth and flicked it over and over with his tongue. She wanted to come, wanted to feel his mouth, his teeth, take her, but she held back. She wanted it to last, to go on forever. When he moved his fingers into her, slowly in and out of her, stretching her, she moaned deep in her throat. She began to undulate, riding his tongue and mouth even as she felt him spreading her ass cheeks. When his fingers found her tiny rosebud she knew if he pushed into her she would come apart. When he whispered through her mind, never taking his mouth from her body, she knew that she was going to shatter.

"I'm going to take you here soon. Fill you here like I do when I'm deep in your pussy, your heat. I want to pound my cock deep in your ass and feel your body tighten around me when you come. Do you want to come, Tess? Do you want to fill my mouth with your cum? Come, love, come now."

Her body responded to his command like he owned it which, she realized, he did.

She screamed loud and long. Her throat ached with it, her ears rang. When he sank his teeth into her flesh just above her clit she came again, his fingers fucking her hard and fast even as he pulled on her with his mouth.

He fed from her, drinking deep from her as he had from her pussy. His cock ached and pulsed with need. Sealing the tiny wounds, he picked her up in his arms and carried her to the bed. Holding her upright, he took off her shirt and laid her back, settling her in the center of the bed.

Standing over her, he slowly took off his clothes and looked down at her. She was the most beautiful creature he had ever seen. Her skin was glistening now with a fine sheen of sweat from her climaxes. Her eyes had darkened to a deep color and her fangs, small and pointed, were bright against her pink lips. He wanted to drop onto her and take her like an animal, and he knew that she would welcome him, but he wanted to make love to her slowly, savor her touch and smell, the texture of her skin and hair.

"Nathaniel, I have to tell you something. I love you. I've never loved before, I know that now. But I do love you with all my heart."

"I love you as well, Tessa. You have my heart also."

Time seemed to stand still for him as he moved to the bed. When he moved between her legs she opened wide and took him in. They fit, their bodies belonged together and as he slid home into her heat he felt something awaken inside.

He was overwhelmed with emotion and something more, something strong and something hers. He looked at her and she was smiling.

"It's my heritage. You are now fae too. Your love set it free and I could give it to you. You are now what I could be if I was whole. I love you, Nathaniel."

As his mouth slanted over hers, he moved into her. He rocked into her slowly at first then stronger and harder. With each movement he felt more of her pour into him. When his balls tightened and his cock filled he surged forward and spilled his seed into her, touching her womb and making her his.

His body was drained, sated, and fed; he fell forward onto her, rolling at the last minute so that he would not crush her with his weight. After pulling her body over his, finding the blanket and throwing that over the two of them, he closed his eyes and slept.

Chapter Seventeen

They had decided that Nathaniel would not be a part of the troop, at least not today. He did not know the signals and he did not know the men. If they lived through this he was going to need to start training with her men as soon as possible.

It was six o'clock that morning. She and Shamus were standing in the deep forest waiting for the summon that would take them to yet another realm, this one far beneath the caves of Avalone.

"I hope you know what you're doing. And that not telling your mate is just as dangerous as what you are about to do." Shamus had told her this eight times already and he was giving her a headache.

"I do. And don't forget that Nathaniel went to Athropos without telling me. Besides, you know as well as I do that Lucas won't see me with people around he doesn't know. And I need to see him."

"Yeah, I know all that. But you weren't mated then and you two are now. There's a big difference once you're mated. He is still going to be pissed off. And when he's done chewing your ass, you know that Athropos will as well."

"Who are you pissing off now, Lady Tessa? Besides me, that is. Lord Shamus, you look as delicious as ever. Are you nearly ready to take your place in the larger scheme of things? Or are you still waiting for the lady to take notice of you?"

Tess and Shamus both dropped their eyes to the floor as soon as Lord Lucas made his presence known to them. Without his permission to look him in the face, Lucas could ensnare a being and claim them as one of his minions. Neither of them wanted to work for the demon lord.

"I'm more than ready, Lord Lucas, but it seems my lady is not. My master Tess has a need to speak with you, sir. I am only along as her support."

"Humm, I wonder about that. Tessa, love, come sit with me and we'll talk. It has been too many years and this boon I owe you needs to be paid. I don't like owing anyone, as you well know. Tell me, what has you coming to me at such a horrible hour?"

She walked to the large sofa and sat in the middle of it. Tess thought that if she sat anywhere else he would think she was being rude. Sitting in the middle gave him the advantage, she knew, but she also knew that he would not press her with Shamus here with her. She was relieved when he sat at the far end and did not touch her.

"I wish to speak to you as equals, Lord Lucas—face to face as it were." Tess held her breath. He would ask her for something in return for this. She only hoped that she got to offer something rather than him ask for it.

"You ask for a lot, Tessa. What will I receive in return? Something worthy, I hope." He had always called her by her full first name. She hated it, but thought now would not be a good time to quibble about it as she had in the past.

"I believe so, sir. I give you information about Marlus and his plans to overpower the Queen of Magick."

Tess heard him shift on the couch and saw his long leg stretch out on the cushion between them. She did not look at him; he had not given his permission.

"You may be my equal—for the moment. Marlus has been talking about taking over the queen's realm since that moron of a mate of hers tried to take her out. He is no closer to it than I am to getting to fuck your man-at-arms here. You must do better than that, I'm afraid. What will you give me as a boon?" He reached out and curled a strand of her hair around his finger. She wanted to pull away, but did not.

Tess licked her lips. This is it, she thought. If he knew what information she had she was dead. If not, then…

"He has help, sir. Albadar is helping him. And also a member of the queen's own council. They plot to overthrow her and then kill off the royal court. I have it on good authority that he plans to do it very soon."

"And this 'authority,' is this person someone you trust, someone I would trust through you?"

"Yes, my lord, it is I. I overheard the councilman and Marlus talking about their plans quite by accident in the Caves of Avalone."

"And Albadar's involvement, how do you know that he is going to help Marlus? How do you know that he isn't merely a pawn in the plan and not a player at all?"

Now came the really tricky part. She had to tell Lucas what she was and how she knew. Not knowing if he would believe her was what she was worried about most. "I took his blood as a pledge of alliance. I also know what he is and his relationship to you, my lord." Tess did not turn to see Shamus, but she could feel his anger as it boiled into her through their connection.

She had not told him what she had done, nor had she told Nathaniel. She knew what she had done was both stupid and dangerous, but he had pledged himself to her and she hoped that by doing so she would be able to control him.

Lucas looked at her sharply with narrowed eyes. She was both relieved and terrified at the same time. His temper was legendary.

"Go on."

Tess stood to pace and looked back at the demon. She needed to walk to talk and when he waved at her with his hand she began walking.

"Albadar has been feeding Marlus fae blood. As you know, fae blood to a de…to one such as yourself makes them powerful for a while, but it will eat at their brain until they are insane. Or, in this case, insaner. Over the past several days six of my men have come down with flulike ailments. When I searched their minds I found that their memories had been altered. When I was able to dig a little deeper I saw that Albadar had lead them to Marlus and then he…they used my men for not only food, but for sexual release."

He got up to the fireplace and threw several logs into the high flames. The room was already too warm; the heat coming from the fire was nearly unbearable. Tess could feel the sweat begin to trickle down her spine. Looking at Shamus she noticed that he was not faring any better.

"This is against the treaty that we have with the queen. They are both aware of this. He faces death—both of them, for breaking it. I'll see them punished immediately." Lucas got up to pace as she had done. Then after a few minutes he settled in the large arm chair closest to the fire and regarded her.

"If you would be so kind, sir, I would rather you hear my plan first. This plan, with your help, will put you into better graces with the queen and you will also set an example to other demons that would go against you. I would consider this a favor to me and will wipe our debt clear."

He stared at her for several minutes. She had stopped pacing when he had stood to do so and now she looked at him as well. Her men would be meeting soon and she wanted to be there, but this was more important.

"Tell me your plan, Tessa, and I will go along with you if it suits me. If you are wrong…"

"I'm not."

"If you are wrong, I will take you, mate or not."

Taking a deep breath Tess nodded and sat down to tell the Lord Demon what she wanted.

~~~

At ten minutes until nine the Fates shimmered into the Great Hall in Molavonta, the castle of Melody, the Queen of Magic. Tess and Shamus had arrived only seconds before they had. Both were dressed in their full armament, but only Tess was there when Athropos nodded to her to go.

Tess stood with two dozen men that were visible to the general assembly room. Albadar was there as well, but he was not aware of the hidden thousands that moved around him. So far so good, Tess thought.

Shamus was with the other more than one thousand men shadowed around the queen's throne room. Colin and Aaron were outside with the rest—nearly six thousand more men, vampires, knights and demons.

Tess had even assigned a dozen men to protect Lord Lucas. Though he had claimed he did not need them he allowed them to follow him to show his faith in Tess, he told her.

When the double oak doors opened her men and she, helmeted and fully armed, escorted the Fates into the room. They encircled the women and walked with Tess in the lead. The room tightened with their combined magic and then settled down after a few seconds.
~~~

As predicted, Councilman Douglass Trundle rose and began to protest the armament the Fates had dared to bring into the great hall.

"Ladies, we are not at war. There is no need for such a show of force. I would very much appreciate you dismissing your guard so that we may proceed with this hearing."

"You may proceed, but these men are not leaving," Clothos said as she sat with her sisters.

Tess smiled behind her helmet. She may not like these women most of the time, but she certainly loved their style.

Douglass moved forward toward the Fates and Tess drew on him, her sword at his heart. He stopped dead and tried to look at her through the slit in her faceguard. She did not say a word and when he did not move back she pressed the blade into him, not breaking the skin, but coming very close. She knew the moment he came to realize that the men beside her had come to the ready, blades drawn and all pointed at him, and they would not back down until he stepped back.

"I only meant to have a private word with the Fates. I meant no harm to anyone, my Lady Knight."

"Then back the fuck up before I have to kill you." Her voice was low and sharp, but Tess knew he had heard. The man backed up so quickly that he nearly tripped over his own feet.

"Shall we please get this over with? I would like to make a…" Marlus started to say in a voice that sounded bored and someone whiny.

"Wait! I have a…I am still the queen of these proceedings. I would like to give a boon to one of the Knights of Avalone. Tessa May, please come forward and to me."

Tess tensed. What the hell? she thought. She was not even aware that the queen even knew she was there. Sword still drawn, she turned and looked at the Fates. Not good, they were smiling. She looked at the now closed doors and wondered if she could make it before anyone could catch her.

"Don't you dare run. So help me, Tess, if I have to chase you down I'll spank you harder than I already plan to. I'm looking forward to pinking up that nice ass of yours. Oh yeah, I know all about your meeting with a demon lord, so that beautiful ass is already mine. If you make me chase you and bring you back you won't sit down for a week," Nathaniel whispered through her mind.

She looked over at him and saw him raise his brow. Shit, she thought, he would do it too.

"Tessa May?" the queen asked again.

"Yes. Yes, I'm here." Tess put her sword back into the scabbard and walked slowly to the dais. Her feet felt leaded and her heart was pounding.

The queen was standing and Tess marveled again at the beauty of the woman before her. When dressed as she was now—cape, gown, crown, and scepter, Tess thought she looked regal and powerful. When Tess was standing before her Mel smiled.

"Take off your headgear. I like to look into the face of the person I'm talking to."

"I'm sorry, my lady, but I cannot—at least not without help. I will need some assistance if you wish it off and I would rather you allow me to leave it in place, please. The gear is clasped in the rear and is very heavy for one person to lift."

"Nathaniel, please come forward, your mate needs your help. She will have a hissy fit, no doubt, if I try to help her."

Nathaniel was suddenly in front of her, dressed as one of her men minus the head gear and the swords. He did carry a gun, a Glock forty with two extra clips and one in the chamber he had told her. She had tried to tell him she would make sure he was safe, but he kissed her and put the gun into the waistband of his leathers.

Looking at him now, this close, and her body already tense and waiting for action, she had to admit he did look good in the pants that fit him like a glove. It was everything she could do not to run from the room with him and find a nice private area. She felt Shamus shift inside of her mind and quickly thought of something else.

She kneeled down on one knee and braced herself for the dismounting, what it was called when a person was disarmed. She knew that Nathaniel knew how to remove it. He had helped her to put it on when they were back at Avalone Castle.

The clasps in the rear went from her neck to the crown at the top of her head. There were six steel buckles that snapped together and fit into the cowl of the chainmaille collar she had on as well. He moved the collar out of his way as he got to the bottom and then unwound the chain from her throat to unstrap the chin guard that held the helmet to her head during battle. The headgear was heavy, weighing in at more than five pounds of pounded steel and leather. It did not seem all that much, but with all the other gear she wore, the bulk of it added to her already weighty protection. It was very hot as well.

Standing again with Nathaniel beside her she looked up at the queen. There were tears in the queen's eyes.

"You've been avoiding me, Tessa May," Mel whispered to her gently.

Tess did not say anything; there would be little point to answer. They both knew it was true and they both knew why. They had both lost so much and had said more, Tess wondered if they would ever be able to put it behind them.

The queen put her hand to her mouth and seemed to be thinking about something. Tess wanted to pace and she nearly did when the queen slapped her. Hard.

Tess's head jerked to the side. She felt her lip open and blood pour freely from the wound. She did not touch the wound, nor did she wipe at the blood that now stained her vest. The room rumbled with voices and restless movement. Her men were moving toward her and the queen.

Not taking her eyes from the queen, Tess stopped them from surging forth by her voice and a simple rising of her hand. "Hold, please."

The queen stepped toward Tess and she stood her ground. She had no idea what this was about, but she was sure that she would find out when this thing was over.

"You always were the most stubborn woman I have ever had the pleasure of knowing. Do you know what this is?"

Tess only stared at the queen. Anger poured from Tess and she nearly didn't look at what the queen was holding in her hand. When the queen nodded down to indicate where she wanted Tess to look she looked down at the chain in the queen's hand. It did not look like much and, as Tess did not wear jewelry, she couldn't figure out what it was, so even it if were expensive or worthy she would not know what its worth would be or why it seemed important to the queen. It wasn't until Mel shifted her fingers that Tess saw them. Her gaze jerked to the queen's.

"Yes, I see that you do. Good." The queen opened the bracelet and gestured towards Tess's hand. She lifted it without thinking. "I've preformed my part in this; all you need to do is accept. Do you know how to do that?"

Tess nodded, still not able to speak past the pounding of her heart. The queen stepped back and sat in her chair. When Tess felt a nudge at her arm she turned and looked at Nathaniel, who was still holding her helmet.

Dropping to her knee again, she waited as he put her hood back on her head and then he stepped up behind the queen's chair. Tess was all the way back to the Fates before she could think.

"Thank goodness we had to wait for that. I'm not sure I would have been able to sleep tonight wondering if the queen was going to bitch slap some broad and then give her a worthless piece of finery. Woo! If we could get back to the real reason we are here, please. I wish to bring my complaint to the council that Queen Melody, Mistress of Light, Keeper of Magic is in violation of her own decree. She is not only an unbound queen, but she is also childless. I protest that she is not fit for the position as queen, and hereby ask to be made king to her queen," Marlus said. Sarcasm was thick in his voice and Tess tried to focus on his words, but they kept swirling around the queen and how she had hit her.

The room was silent for several heartbeats then all hell broke loose. Shouting and accusations started, some moved toward the dais, the queen, and Nathaniel. With a quick command the Knights moved to protect the Brianals.

A shrill whistle sounded several times to try and gain attention, but it was the gunshot going off that silenced the room completely. Tess glanced at Nathaniel, who was smiling. He and the queen were covered in plaster dust, but both of them were fine.

"My lady, he is correct. I'm afraid that I have no choice but to recommend that he be made your mate, effective at sunset tonight," Councilman Trundle stated.

Tess was sure that he was trying to sound remorseful, but all he did was sound ridiculous.

"Wow! Just like that, huh? He complains and without any deliberation, you decree it as fact. I don't think so; I'm going fight this all the way."

"With what, Mel? You have no guard—well, none to speak of really. What do you have, like fifty, a hundred men?

Do you think that this woman you just hit is going to come to your rescue? You just hit her before several hundred beings. If anything, she'll probably come to my side if I ask her. If you would care to look outside you'll see that I have three thousand men who are all ready, willing, and able to fight until their deaths for me," Marlus said with a sneer.

"Actually, I have the men. You have nothing. Thank you, Marlus, for setting this up for me. I'll take over for now. I have suddenly found that I have no more use for you or your fucking whiny ways," Albadar said as he moved out of the line of the guard.

They all watched as Albadar pulled a blade from behind his back and plunged it into Marlus' chest. Shock moved through the room.

Tess did not think an underlord could be killed easily, so she knew that the blade must have been cursed. She also knew that the underlord Marlus would not be returned to his lord until the blade was removed.

"Albadar, what is the meaning of this? This man had a complaint; you can't just come into these proceedings and kill him. I was about to make a judgment," Douglass shouted over the din. He was nervous, his voice was shaky, and Tess knew that he did not know that Albadar was going to kill him as well.

"Shut up, you moron. When I am king, you are one of the first to go. I'm going to be the most powerful king ever named. Others will fear me; I will be honored and revered by all. And you, Queen of Magic, you will be my greatest gift to myself."

Tess moved to be in front of the queen. She wanted to be close to the dais to protect Nathaniel if need be and to protect the queen if this idiot got too close. The queen may yet be a true immortal, but she still could be hurt.

"What of Lord Lucas? Don't you think he might want to get a little piece of this pie too?" Tess asked as she nodded to the men to her left. Things were about to go bad very fast.

"He is the first name on my list. He will not even know what is going on until I have his black beating heart in my fist. Melody, take my hand and come with me willingly and I may not kill your family right away."

When Albadar reached out his hand Tess turned to the queen. She looked at Nathaniel and he nodded at her. Tess dropped before the queen and said, "I serve you willingly, my queen."

Chapter Eighteen

Nothing happened at first. Nathaniel wanted to go to her, to Tess, but he was not sure what was happening. Just as he stepped forward, she threw back her head and moaned as if in great pain. Taking another step toward her, he felt the first pain shoot through his head and he stopped. Before he could question what had happened, pain ripped through him and had him dropping to his knees on the floor in agony.

His head felt tight then it seemed to expand and he wrapped his hands around it to try and hold it together, for he was sure it was splitting in two. He felt blood begin to pour from his nose, his mouth; his fangs elongated and stretched in his mouth then spilled to the floor beneath him glistening brightly in the pool of his blood.

The pain started in his back just below his neck, and he tried to turn to see if anyone was stabbing him. Because of the pain that radiated from there he was sure that was what was happening. He tried to move, to dislodge whatever it was, but his belly began to burn and he leaned forward on his hands to throw up, to try and expel whatever was making him hurt. But what he saw made him forget everything for a moment.

His hands began to morph; his claws, a part of what he was, began to extend from his fingers and then simply move beyond the tips to lie next to his fangs. The pain might have been extraordinary, but he could not feel it yet. His mind was overwhelmed and could not grasp what was happening. Next, he noticed that the skin along his wrists began to bleed. Wide strips of flesh began to redden and become raw; blood poured from these fresh wounds as he was, what felt like, being flayed alive. As whatever it was moved up his arms and over his elbows, his hot blood covered his fingers and began to run in a thick red stain down the dais he was still on and to the floor below.

He was going to die. Whatever was happening, he was dying from it and he needed to tell Tess, tell her that he loved her. Darkness started to tighten around his vision, his hearing had become muted, his voice raw from his screams. Before he was no longer able to hold onto consciousness he threw back his head and said the only thing that had been running through his mind that made sense. "Tess, I love you."

~~~

The room rippled hard, expanding and stretching to seemingly make room for more of something yet to come, to be revealed.

Tess dropped to her knees when the first sharp pain assaulted her. Her shoulders pulled and her scapulas moved, morphing into something hard and wide. Tess leaned forward, her head touching the floor, just as the first part of the transformation began. Out of the corner of her eye she could see Nathaniel, could see his pain and blood. She wanted to go to him, to comfort him, but could not. She needed to let her change happen so that she could protect them all.

Along her back large nodes pushed through her vest. As it began to grow something burst from the skin and the material
~~~

of her leather vest formed around it, shielding her body from exposure.

Stretching out her arms wide, they seemed to duplicate and separate until long wings formed and unfurled from her, opening and expanding. Their translucent colors, bright in the room as they flashed along the walls, sparkled against the people in the room and the walls and floor. As the colors solidified and her wings became translucent yet still bright, she turned and rose from the floor. As power poured from the wings the colors deepened; reds became brighter, hues of greens and blues filled in where yellows and orange raced to color the area. Fully erect, Tess spread her wings, opening them wide and then wider still.

Her face changed as well. Her ears elongated and now had a hint of a point at the tips. Jewels, rubies and emeralds, filled the crown that encircled her head, marking her as a Master Fae, the last of her race.

Fluttering her wings once, she rose from the floor a few feet and then dropped back again. She smiled at Albadar.

"No! That's not possible. You're dead. I made sure you were all dead. I worked with that idiot, Sherman. He knew what he was supposed to do. I told him how to make you all mortal, but he didn't kill his mate. He said she was unconscious so she was safe, but the Black Knights, you were all there, all dead."

"You knew Sherman? You were the power source and the trainer for his magic, weren't you?" the queen asked, though it sounded as if she already had her answer.

"Of course I was. You don't think that fool was smart enough to figure this out on his own, did you? Christ, even Trundle was duped for a time. How do you think we knew so much? Sherman was feeding us information for centuries about your family. Then when the half wonder Sherman came along we had our way of getting rid of you once and for all. But he got greedy. I was happy to hear that you got rid of him for me. So thank you for that."

Tess shook her head. He sounded so sincere that she thought that Albadar was mad. "You know that what you are doing is against the treaty with your kind, and especially against Lord Lucas?" Tess had figured out what Albadar was when she took his alliance the other day.

"And you are supposed to be dead. But I do plan to remedy that right now." When he lunged forward he grabbed the queen with his jeweled dagger in his hand. Nathaniel screamed at that moment, screamed his love for Tess as he fell forward into his blood. It was the perfect distraction Albadar needed and he hid himself behind the queen.

Tess grinned as she moved toward him. She opened her wings as she moved and brought her sword forward; it was steady and true. "You are going to die, Albadar. It will be slow and it will be painful, unless you release my queen right now."

"Release her? I think not, fae. She will be my queen and I her king. Then I will kill you both, starting with your mate here. I have not come alone. I have your men surrounded and now you will see the power of me."

The room shimmered to life suddenly. Every warrior, fae or other being, materialized around the room. Each of them held a demon in his clutches, a blade to his throat. The doors burst open and the room filled with more men, more warriors.

"My lady, your call," Tess said without taking her blade from her position at the ready.

"Stop! I've seen enough." Lord Lucas stepped to the dais and raised his hand. Albadar froze instantly. "You've been a bad boy, Albadar. What am I to do with you, do you think?" Tess could see the panic in Albadar's eyes.

"Sire, have you only just arrived? Good, your timing, as usual, could not have been better. I was playing with Marlus until you arrived. You can see that things did not go as I had planned. I had to protect myself from this madwoman. Why, she even professes to be a warrior fae, if you can believe that. She believes herself to be better than you. I wanted to bring the two of them, both her and Marlus, before you so that you could be the one to punish then, but things went wrong and I had to save the queen from them and he had to be killed."

His sentences began to run together in his haste to explain. Lord Lucas merely waited, his arms crossed over his chest. "Is that the story you're sticking with? It's a very poor one if you ask me. Lady Tess, I thank you for your warning and your help. Queen Melody, what say you concerning this? I will abide by your wishes." He bowed before her, a simple bending at the waist, but an act of trust, for Shamus had his blade pointed at the lord's back even as Lucas moved to the dais.

"I would be able to think better if this moron did not have me clutched so tightly to his vile stench," Mel said, her voice heavy with sarcasm and scorn.

Suddenly she was released. Albadar, however, was still frozen in place. With a nod from Tess her men moved forward and wrapped him in chains that had been warded with magic, both black and white. He would not be able to escape at all now.

"Thank you, Lord Lucas. I was not aware that you were in attendance. Maybe next time you are within my walls someone could inform me, Tess. As far as Albadar, you are aware that he has broken our treaty, but…"

"My lady, you cannot believe anything this man has said to…" Councilman Trundle squeaked.

"Silence! As I was saying, our treaty has been broken by him. But I can see that he has had help. Perhaps…I'm thinking that both men have worked together and that they both would be better served to follow you, Lord Lucas, to do with as you see fit. I trust you know of something these two can do to keep them out of trouble for awhile, don't you?"

"Yes, my lady, I like the way you think. Both men, you say? I believe I have the perfect job for them. I believe that one shall be a service, the other serviceable. I believe they will be perfect as the outlet for sexual pleasure or displeasure for my men."

Tess still had not moved, her sword never wavering or shaking. She had noticed that the councilman had sighed heavily and Tess could not figure out why no one could see his involvement in this when, suddenly, he disappeared. Tess looked at Lucas and he winked at her before turning to Albadar.

"You almost fooled me, Albadar. Almost would have too without the intervention of Lady Knight here. Unless, of course, you have thought up another version of what really happened here? Perhaps you need time to come up with yet another one. I can arrange that if Master Tessa will allow me to take you with me. Tessa?" Lord Lucas smiled at her and she shuddered. Whatever his plans for Albadar were, they would be long and painful.

"No! I mean, no, I should stay here. I need to be judged here. Queen Melody should have that boon," Albadar said before Tess could speak.

Lucas merely looked at Albadar then he bowed before the queen. When he straightened he handed her a bunch of blood red roses. "My lady. I would first like to tell you how much I appreciate you allowing me to watch the proceedings of this...let's call it an event, shall we? Your emissary came to me to let me know what this man has done to you and yours. I was not aware of how much his involvement was in your loss both now and before. You have my deepest apologies."

"Lord Lucas, the treaty is broken, perhaps you and I could come up with a better one, more, how shall I say, helpful to us both."

"I believe I would like that. Yes, I would like that very much. Why don't we adjourn to your chamber where we can be more comfortable with our…talk."

Tess started forward and was stopped by Shamus. He pointed his blade at the demon lord's throat and pressed forward just enough to break his skin. Blood welled at the tiny wound. "I think not. Back away or I will remove you from this realm. Permanently."

The demon looked at Shamus and, with a quick bow, he stood and threw back his head and laughed. "So, you make your move, Lord Shamus?"

"Never mind. It's time for you to go."

"As you wish. For now at least." And Lord Lucas snapped his fingers.

Tess did not wait for the outcome of what looked to be a major pissing contest, but gathered Nathaniel into her arms. "Shamus, I leave you in charge. If you need me it had better be a matter of life and death…well, you know what to do." With that, she disappeared from the room.

Chapter Nineteen

"…again I will not be responsible for how badly I will hurt you. You told me that two days ago and then again yesterday and, if I'm not mistaken, you told me again this morning. If he does not wake soon I will have to fill in my time waiting for him to do so by peeling your fingernails off from your hands one at a time. I would suggest that you…"

"Tess, don't hurt the man, please? I think there has been enough bloodshed this week, don't you?" Nathaniel felt the bed shift then, suddenly, she was sitting next to him. He did not hurt, not really, but he was weak. He could barely lift his arm to touch her and left it lay when it proved too much.

"You scared the hell out of me, you arrogant ass. You were not supposed to change yet. But not you! Oh no, you just had to do it right then, didn't you? Then, to top it all off, you had to be out of it for six days to boot. Well, I certainly hope you got enough rest because you will not see this bed for a very long…for a very long…I hate you, you bastard. I thought you were dying on me. Please don't do that again." When he laid her body next to his he wrapped his arm around her waist.

He reached up, surprised at how much stronger he felt, brushed away her tears and pulled her tighter to his chest. He kissed her head as the others moved out of the room.

Six days? He had been out of it for six day? And she had said changed. He had been changed into what? he wondered. He thought about the pain he had felt and the blood, and his body covered in a sheen of sweat.

"It's over now, Nathaniel. I've got you. You're safe now." Tess was cooing at him as she rubbed his chest.

"You said I changed. Changed what?" He could remember his blood and lifted his arm up to look at it.

Bands of markings covered his arm from his wrist up to where his shirt covered the rest of his arm. The colors were dark and rich—reds, blues, and golds. Some of the writing was in hieroglyphics, others in designs, and still more in words he could understand. They told a story, a long tale of warriors and their service to the queen. He stiffened when he realized he could read all the languages as well at the glyphs.

"It's our lineage. Your markings were so painful because there were centuries of information to imprint on your skin. From now on it won't hurt as bad and it will be quicker too." She sat up again, pulled the blanket down his chest, and ran her hand over him. Sitting up on his elbows he looked down at his torso.

The marks were all along his left side and down to his navel. When he touched his hand to one grouping, it felt both cool and hot. "Every time we go to battle or something happens, it will be noted on our skin."

"Vampires can't tat, Tess. We heal too quickly and the ink is rejected. I've tried before to get one. The tat that I have from before I changed to vamp is still there, but no new ones will stay. How did you manage it?"

He watched her face and saw confusion there. He looked at her arm and noticed she too was marked – identical to his.

"You're not a vampire anymore. In order for us to bar…"

"What? What do you mean I'm not a vamp anymore? What the fuck did you do to me?" He got off the bed and backed away from it and her.

"There wasn't any time for me to explain. Our queen was…"

"She isn't my queen. What. Did. You. Do? And how the hell can you change me back? Whatever you've done, you'll undo it right fucking now. I want my vampirism back today." When she reached for him, he jumped back away from her again.

He watched as she got up off the bed and picked up her boots. When he thought she was not going to help him she started talking again as she pulled them on. "I'll send Shamus by and he can help you with things until I get back. The queen is the only one who can…repair what you feel I've done to you. You can eat now, by the way, and there is food in the kitchen. That bowl of stone by the bed are fairies and if you need me, send one of them to find me." She stood now and his heart constricted. Something had happened here and he was not sure what he had done.

"Tess, I…"

"If you just give me a couple of days I'm sure I can get things straightened out to your satisfaction." And then she was gone.

She could not have been gone for more than a few seconds when someone knocked on the front door. Nathaniel walked through the house and opened it to slam it shut again on Shamus.

Nathaniel jumped back from the sunlight filling the room. He heard the fae on the other side of the door chuckle and

Nathaniel realized too late that the sun would not harm him anymore.

"Sorry. Come in. Old habits," Nathaniel said as he opened the door again.

"No worries, Lord Knight. That's what I'm here for, to help you learn the ropes."

Nathaniel started for the kitchen. His stomach was rumbling for the first time in centuries. He spoke over his shoulder as he went. "So, I take her name now rather than the other way around?" He noticed the other man raise his brow and flushed when he realized how chauvinistic he sounded.

"No, sire, that is your title. Knight or Warrior, both apply to you and many will call you one or the other. Is there something wrong?"

"And what do they call her?" He decided to ignore the question, at least for the moment.

"Some call her just Tess, others Lady Tess. Depends, I suppose. During work or a need, she is always Master, as you will be. What would you like to be called, sire?"

Nathaniel was opening cabinets and closing them without removing anything. When he opened the large refrigerator he was shocked to find the shelves full. He turned to Shamus. "I haven't a clue how to cook any of this stuff. She got her panties in a serious twist and left without explaining to me how she plans to turn me back to a vampire. She then tells me you're coming to explain things and, oh by the way, there's a bowl of fairies and to send one to get her if I need her. It's a bowl of rocks. Pretty rocks, but still, it's just rocks."

Without saying a word, Shamus left the room. Great, Nathaniel thought, I've managed to piss off another one and I still can't eat. When Shamus returned with the bowl in question and set it on the table, Nathaniel was beyond grateful.

But he did not say anything. He planned to be gone before much longer anyway and he did not need any more friends.

Shamus shoved him into a chair. Moving to the cabinets, he pulled down a large box with some cartoon characters on it and, in another cabinet, he pulled out a large bowl.

"Pick up a rock, Lord Knight. It doesn't matter which one for now, just pick one."

Blindly reaching into the bowl of stones Nathaniel pulled out a yellow one and held it out to Shamus. Nathaniel watched as the fae poured some of the contents from the box into the bowl and filled it. His "breathe on it" was slightly muffled when he bent over into the fridge and pulled out the milk. He sat down across from Nathaniel and set the bowl in front of him.

Whatever it was, it was bright and smelled very sweet. He watched as Shamus poured milk into it and was startled when he pressed a spoon at him.

"Just breathe on it, the stone," he said again.

"What's supposed to happen, a genie pops out and rips out my throat?" Nathaniel flushed again. He was not sure what was wrong with him, but he felt that having his life taken from him could justify some of it.

"No, sire. That one you're holding is a yellow fairy. She is the stone, breathe."

Nathaniel heard the tone, but again decided to ignore it for now. He rubbed his thumb over the smooth, warm surface and dipped his spoon into the bowl of food at the same time. He puffed a breath across the brightly-colored stone and began to eat. He was just putting the spoon into his mouth when the stone began to change.

Wings began to separate from the smoothness. Tiny and bright, they began to extend up and out from his palm. Her face was next, eyes formed, a nose began to take shape, then lips and her chin appeared. When the column of her neck started to emerge, he saw her wings flutter and legs begin to mold and tiny feet move. Her toes began to wiggle and she looked over at him and smiled. When she leaned back he saw breast and waist as she seemed to rest across is fingers.

Nathaniel looked at Shamus and saw him lean back in his chair as if nothing out of the ordinary was happening right in the palm of Nathaniel's hand.

Soon she was standing, her wings moving back and forth as the sunlight reflected off them. While her wings looked like whatever one thought a fairy would look like, that was where the similarities ended.

She was about six inches tall and her hair was a bright daffodil color that was short and streaked with bright green. Her tiny shirt was a t-shirt from a band that Nathaniel had never heard of and her jeans were worn and full of holes. And she had on flip-flops. Her tiny toes were painted black, as were her fingernails. She was also sporting a nasty, pissed off look on her face.

"If you woke me up just to gawk, then I'm going to give you a horrible belly ache." Her voice, while small, was not soft at the moment.

"Daniy, this is the Master Tess's mate, Lord Nathaniel. Nathaniel, meet Daniy, a daffodil fairy. She wakes the bulbs in the spring."

The little being in his hand dropped to her knees and her head bounced off his finger. "I'm truly sorry, Master Nathaniel. I wasn't aware she had finally…that Lady Tess had been…fuck a duck."

"Perhaps now would be a good time to shut up, Daniy. Master Nathaniel requires a cook, someone to fill his belly and clean up afterwards. Could you go and find one for him post haste?"

"Yes, sire. 'Twill be my pleasure." And then she was gone.

~~~

Several hours later he was walking around trying to find Tess. He could not reach her through their bond as he kept hitting a wall. And the thought of waking another rock to go find her frankly gave him the willies. He did not mind the awakening, what Shamus had called it. It was the terror he felt from them when they realized who he was.

Shamus had told him that he had never known Tess to use a fairy stone so maybe Daniy's previous owner had not been so kind.

He had been walking for about an hour when he saw what he thought was a dragon. The closer he got, the bigger it got until he was a mere dot in the scheme of things.

"You must be the new master. I am Lord Draco Enneahedral. Come and sit for awhile and converse with an old man. It's been ages since a warrior fae male has graced these lands. You must tell me how you are enjoying them," the giant being said to him.

"I'm a vampire, not fae. Well, as soon as she gets me back to being myself, I guess. I'm Nathaniel Tremont."

"Change you back, you say? Why would you want to do that? You're not happy with your mate?" Lord Draco asked, shock in his voice.

"It's not that. She did it without asking me and I liked being a vamp. What am I suppose to do all day as a giant fairy?"

"You can fly with me if you've a mind too. I love to soar through the skies. Makes me feel young again to feel the wind across my wings. How does it feel for you?"

"I can't fly; it's a myth among humans that vampires can fly. We can move really fast, but not fly."
~~~

"But as a fae you can. Your wings are a little weak since you've just gotten them, but I bet you can go far. Let me show you." He watched as the huge beast began to move toward him.

"No! I can't fly, I tell you. I'm a vampire. Not a fae" He felt stupid and embarrassed as soon as he realized how he sounded. He started to apologize, but the dragon went on as though nothing had happened.

"Humm, without asking, you say… that doesn't sound like my Tessa. I wonder what she had been thinking."

"She hadn't. She needed to change and brought me over with her, Shamus said. Then when I tell her to change me back, she disappears. I was trying to find her when I happened upon you."

"If Tess doesn't want to be found, then you won't find her." The dragon chuckled at that as he laid his head down and closed his eyes, a slight smile still on his lips.

It was then that Nathaniel realized he had been speaking to him through his mind. He had never been able to do that before, only with Tess. But as his mate, they would. He started to ask Draco about it when Draco raised his head up again.

"I don't know when her punishment is, do you? I've been asking about it, but no one seems to know just yet. Tess has only just told the queen her choice of punishment. I thought the queen had said it would be one week after you woke, but with you wanting to leave, I wonder if it will be sooner than that."

"Punishment? For what? And I never said I was leaving. I just want to have my life back the way it was."

"I don't know all the details, but something to do with allowing a demon lord into the throne room. I heard she had agreed to the lash. Those are harsh, especially for a woman. The whips come around and dig deep into the tender flesh of their breasts. This time is more than the last time Tess had been beaten for disobeying the queen. The first time, Lord Sherman had given them to her himself. I wonder who they'll get to do it this time."

"Why would she be in trouble for something that saved the queen's life? And why would she agree to something as barbaric as a whip?"

The dragon laid his head back down and seemed to be thinking, his brow furrowed deep with lines.

Whipping. Tess was going to be beaten and she had not told him a single thing. Of course he had not given her a chance to tell him anything, flying off the handle the way he had. But he thought that Shamus should have. Then realized he probably had either been told not to tell him, or assumed that Nathaniel would know.

"It's actually a cat-o-nine tails they'll use on her. The last beating was horrific and had only been a hundred lashes. This time will double that at least. Almost two thousand strokes across her tender back. Shame that, poor girl."

"Two thousand? I thought you said it would only double?" Nathaniel caught himself pacing and wondered if she had done that to him as well, then flushed. Of course she had not.

"Well, each lash will be multiplied by nine correct? Then times the two hundred lashes—that is to say if that's all she receives. Could be more, I guess. Anyway, that could make it as much as eighteen hundred wounds. Poor girl will be lucky if she can move for a week or two. Those kinds of lashes don't heal quickly, the ones given by the queen."

Two thousand or more lashes across her beautiful back. He tried to reach out to her again and hit a wall. How would she stand it and why was the queen making her do it?

"Lord Draco, how to I find the queen?"

“Well, sorry to tell you, but you’d have to use them wings of yours if you want to get there today. Ever been to Molavonta? Well, just think about it and you’ll just go there.”

After a quick and very helpful lesson in extending his wings and flying Nathaniel was off.

Chapter Twenty

"Thank you for seeing me, my queen. I appreciate you taking the time…"

"Cut it out, Tess. What can I do for you? And please tell me you are here to stop this stupidity."

Tess looked at her sharply. Surely word that Nathaniel wanted out had not reached her before she had a chance to tell her. She started pacing. It had taken her the better part of the day to work through the hurt he had given her, then longer to work through her anger. She had nearly killed three of her more experience men and had sent one of them to the infirmary from exhaustion. He had told her he had been honored to serve her in any way she had needed. She wanted to scream.

All her men had their fae given back to them. Each had their wings and more than half were now being paid for their duties. The others would be receiving their "money" as soon as she figured how to pay them.

Fae warriors had no use for money as none of them left the realm where money was used. As member of the Black Knights everything they needed was provided for them—food, clothing, armament, even help around the house if they needed it. They had no need of cars either, of course, and those with families simply had help to get what they needed.

"He wants to be changed back. Nathaniel wants to be changed back to a vamp. He isn't happy with being fae and is demanding I change him back to the way he was before." Tess did not look at the queen. She knew what she would see there, disappointment and disgust, just the way she felt.

"I see. And what did you tell him about his abilities? Is he aware of what he is, what he's capable of as fae? Does he know what happens if I allow him to go back to the human world?"

Tess had hoped she would not ask her this, but knew deep down that she would.

"He…he's not…Nathaniel won't let me touch him. He pulled away when I tried to give it to him." Had she touched him when he was looking at her, everything, all the knowledge and understanding of their kind—no, of her kind—would have been his.

"Tess, look at me."

"I'd rather not, my lady. Give him what he wants, please. I'll have Shamus bring him to you when the time is right. I'd like to go now, if you please?" Her heart was breaking. Actually, she thought it was already broken. Shattered in her chest, leaving an empty space where it had been before.

"Have Shamus bring him by after your punishment. Tess, I ask again for you to reconsider your choice of punishment for bringing Lord Lucas to the realm. Had he not been there things might have gone horribly different for us all and you have to realize that."

"How do you expect my men to follow a leader who thinks she is above the laws they enforce? If there is nothing else, I'll be going."

"You have my permission. Be safe, Tess."

~~~

"Shamus, my punishment is tomorrow at noon. Could you please have Nathaniel brought to the queen sometime tomorrow evening? She will grant his request then," she whispered to his mind.

Tess had transformed to fly as soon as she left the castle. She had been moving along the air streams for ten minutes when she felt she could speak to her friend without him knowing just how upset she was.

"Are you going to talk to him first? Or are you just going to let everything go? He deserves better than this, Tess. You should tell him what you've given him at the very least."

"And what of your mate, Shamus? Is she happy with you right now? Oh wait! She doesn't know you are her true mate, does she? I forgot you hide that knowledge from her as well as you do from yourself. Are you being fair to her? Are you telling her what you can be giving her? When you make yourself known to her, then you can tell me how to handle my own mate. Now have Nathaniel there after the punishment." She closed the connection and dropped to the ground. Her heart was broken, she decided then. It would have to be to hurt his badly.

~~~

Shamus appeared in the house just at daybreak. Nathaniel had been startled and he fell backwards and tripped over an end table. He could feel the anger boiling off the man and Nathaniel felt his back arch in response to the emotion. He wondered if his wings would somehow protect him and let the thought go.

"Come with me. I need a witness and you need to have a conference with the queen. But you speak first or, if things go as planned, you won't have the opportunity to."

"All right." As soon as the words left his mouth and he grabbed Shamus' hand they were in the antechamber of the queen's personal residence.

"Did she see you? No? Good. All right, Nathaniel, let's get you changed. Before I do, I must ask you some questions. Have a seat. Are you enjoying your time here? I hope so. We'll all miss you very much. Especially Lord Draco, he has taken quite a liking to you." The queen moved over to her chair and indicated the other two with a nod of her head as she spoke. Nathaniel sat next to Shamus.

"It's a very beautiful kingdom and if you think to change my mind with this line of questioning then know it won't work. I've used these tactics myself on a criminal. I'm going to be vampire and that's all there is to it."

"Why would I want to change your mind? Tess has called in a favor and I'm granting it for her. I owe her a great deal," the queen said, looking perplexed.

"Whatever." He knew she was trying something on him and it was not going to work. He had been an officer of the law for too long for much to get by him.

"Why do you want to be a vampire again?" The question startled him a little because although he had been saying it all day—he wanted to be changed—no one had asked him why.

"I liked my life the way it was before. I see no reason why I should have to change that to be here."

"But you won't. Be here, I mean. Once you go back to being a vampire you won't be able to return here again. Molavonta does not allow others to come and go."

"What about Avalone? Will we be able to live there?" Tess would be farther away from her work, but being able to fly should help with that.

"I don't think you understand. You'll be back to the way you were before. Which brings me to my next question."

"Why do I get the feeling there is a trick here somewhere? You aren't telling me something. What is it?"

"I have no idea what you mean. Do you want to remember Tess or not? I would suggest not. It'll be hard on you enough, I think, as it is. But that's up to you."

"I would think, as my mate, it would be important that she knows who I am. It will make things less weird when we make love and I need to feed from her, don't you think?" He started to laugh, but realized that she was serious.

Then he noticed the exchange of looks between Shamus and the queen. He knew that without a doubt he was not going to like this.

"Tess will no longer be your mate, Nathaniel. She has to stay here. I cannot release her kind and I cannot lose her to the human race. You will go back—as you have demanded—to the way you were before. In order to do that I'll need to make you human first, then vampire. I cannot allow a vampire, an unmated vampire, in my realm. It wouldn't be safe."

"You lie! Aaron MacManus comes and goes as he pleases. I've seen it with my own eyes."

"I'll give you the benefit of the doubt because you don't know, but I do not lie. I can't. As the holder of all magic, it is impossible for me to tell an untruth. Magic is unstable enough without having a liar at the helm, don't you agree? And Aaron is mated. Mated and happy with what he is and what he is to this realm. Tess will remain here as an advisor to the Black Knights. Your bond will be terminated. Now, I ask again, do you want to remember her or not?" There was steel in her voice, hard and unforgiving.

"There's something else you should know, Nathaniel," Shamus started to say, but the queen cut him off.

"No, Shamus. This is not his to know. He wants his life back and that is not information he needs to make his decision that I have put before him. Well, Nathaniel, what's your answer?"

"What is it, Shamus? What do you feel I need to know about Tess?" He sounded desperate because he was. His heart was hurting. Not to see her again was too much. He could not think beyond this moment.

"Once you leave her she'll become infertile. Our kind can only have children every one hundred years. But because she is the last of her kind, with a mate her ability to become impregnated is every ten years until she has three pair of children. Warrior fae are the strongest beings there are among all beings, and her race will dominate and change whomever her offspring mates with to repopulate the realm. Once she has fulfilled that count she will continue to have children in the normal time frame. If you return to the human world Tess will never have a child."

"Are you saying that she doesn't revert back when I do? And why is she the last anyway? At her age I would think she would have several hundred relatives by now."

"I cannot take her heritage away from her. When I did it the first time her family was still alive. Now they aren't. Fae children can die before they turn twenty-five, at the age of maturity for her kind. Tess's siblings were all murdered by unknown forces, though now I'm sure I know who may have been responsible."

Nathaniel's mind was reeling. He needed a quiet corner to absorb it all in, but he knew the queen wanted her answer too.

He wondered if it was all true and realized that it did not matter. He loved Tess and, even if they took all his memories away about her, he knew that his heart would still have a hole where she had been. He thought of his life without her today and realized that he could not go an entirety without her. He thought about her little house and the yard. He thought about the food he had eaten today and the apple he had pulled off the tree and eaten. The taste of it, amazing and warm. Then the sun on his face and his talk with a dragon.

He then thought about Tess. They fought so much, not about important things, but just fights. And the sex was fantastic. He sobered then. A child. He would not see her grow large with their children. Or see them grow. He would never see Tess hold them, smile at them. He would not wake beside her, hold her in his arms as she suckled their child. Could he give that up? Yes, he realized he could. But did he want too? That was the real question.

"Where is Tess right now?"

"The south field. She is having a bit of a sword play with Lord Draco—in his human form that is. She is exhausted, though. I believe she has bested several of her men today. What sort of frustrations do you suppose she is trying to work off?"

Chapter Twenty One

Tess was worn out. The stress and working her men through their paces on little sleep had her feeling like she had been hit by a car. And then the driver had backed up to have another go at it.

A ripple of magic told her Draco was near. Looking up into the skies Tess could see him swoop across the blue of it and then he disappeared for a few minutes before she heard him coming through the forest. When he cleared the forest—literally—she smiled at him. The woodland nymphs were going to be pissed. Again.

"They told me to do it, Lady Knight. Their leader…I cannot remember his name, could you help an old dragon?" he whispered through her mind.

"Lord Oak, Lord Draco. His name is Lord Oak. He did mention that he needed some help with the forest. I thought he meant the planting." Tess grinned as her men scrambled out of his way.

Draco made a grand entrance when he was in the form of his dragon. She so loved the fact that he cared not that he was leaving lake-sized footprints nor that he was scaring half the forest animals in his wake.

"Ah, yes. Well, he said that he wanted to trim the trees. Do you think that's what he had in mind?" They both looked at the destruction he had caused.

Tess laughed. "I doubt it. And I have a feeling you were aware of that too. What brings you to my field, sire? Besides crushing all manner of trees and flowers?"

Draco shifted to man. A very handsome one at that. But it was his eyes that mesmerized her. The purple of his wings with the flecks of gold—not the color but actual gold sprinkled within them. His hair, also a deep purple shade, hung to his waist, straight as a rod. He looked to be about in his mid-thirties, but she knew him to be more than two thousand years old. His beard, just under his mouth, trimmed neat, was just beginning to gray. His face, scarred from many battles, was beautiful despite that. He grinned at her now.

"Come. Come and fly with me. It has been so long since we have taken to the skies. I know a place where we can fly forever and see the realm as it's meant to be seen."

Tess could feel her exhaustion crushing down on her. Her hurt and anger at Nathaniel as well. She looked to the sky and thought, what could it hurt? In a few hours she'd be taken to the dungeon anyway.

"Okay. But I have to be at Molavonta in two hours. So you have to not let me forget." Like she would be able to. Something about being beaten stuck in one's memory very well.

Walking to the large field behind the trees that Lord Draco had knocked down, he brought Nathaniel up. She didn't want to talk about him, but she didn't want to piss anyone else off today either.

"Nathaniel came to see me. Your mate, he came to see me. I believe he looked for you. Did he? Did he find you, Lady Knight?"

"I didn't want to be found, Lord Draco, as you well know. You have something to say, so say it. I've better things to do with my time than play games with you. We've been friends for far too long to beat around the bushes." Tess stopped and stared up at the sky. "I can't. I can't imagine what he said to you, so out with it."

Tess could feel his gaze. Draco could see so much, she knew. But she also knew that he did things in his own time and not in hers.

"Lord Nathaniel doesn't know of your punishment, does he?"

"He doesn't know, or he didn't know? Not that it matters, but no, he didn't. He's decided…he'll be gone before it matters, if it ever did." Tess hurt again. And having someone know of her failure hurt more. "I'm too tired, I think, after all. Some other time, perhaps? I have things I need to do before—"

"Come, Tess, please? Fly with me. It won't be long now before I'm no longer a part of this world or any other. I would love another chance to soar with you, my dear."

"Don't, Lord Draco. Please, let's not talk about death today. I beg of you. When my life is finished, I too will be the last of my kind. So for today, let's not talk about such things," Tess begged him.

Neither said another word as they came to the open field, each of them so deep in thought that they barely noticed the beauty of the forest and the trees and flowers. They hardly noticed the lake and its sliver eddies along its otherwise smooth service. When they shifted, both of them a huge dragon, Draco took to the skies first, his beauty and style lost on the warrior fae still on the ground. When Tess took to the skies minutes later it was with a heavy heart and broken dreams.

They played for over two hours. Draco had been soaring around to bat the large boulder back to Tess when she saw the guard coming onto the field. The time had come. Signaling to Draco, she dropped gently to the ground and shifted even as Draco moved away.

"Lady Tessa Knight, by order of the Queen of Magic, I…I…please, my lady, don't do this. You've saved us all. I don't want to—"

"Buck up, man. Right now! What do you think you're doing? This is the right of the law. Should I hold myself above them because of the way the day turned out? No, I cannot. I broke the law that governs us all. I alone took a demon lord into the queen's chambers. Had you done the same thing, do you think I would have cut you any slack?"

"No, my lady. But you—"

"Enough, George. She's made her decision and so has the queen." Shamus appeared suddenly and cuffed Tess's hand. "You sure about this?" he asked quietly.

"You know that I am." Tess looked at George again. "Stand down. And for going against me in front of your men I want you to spend the remainder of the week in your home. If I catch you about, I'll have you mucking stalls for six months. Do I make myself clear?"

George looked ready to protest, but a raised brow from her and his mouth snapped shut. She knew that he'd rather die than to disobey her, and keeping him away from her sentencing would keep him from doing something really stupid.

"Yes, my lady. I shall go now. Lord Shamus."

After he left the field Shamus finished putting the cuffs at her ankles. When he stood he looked her in the eye. "He would have broken, I believe. He would have never been the same had he seen you whipped. I believe the young guard is quite smitten with you. You were smart to send him back. We would have lost a good man if you hadn't."

Tess looked away. "I don't know what you're talking about. Let's get going."

They were walking to the stream when Shamus spoke again. She thought she'd be able to stand twice the lashings if he wouldn't tell her again how stupid she was for doing this. But he surprised her.

"I would ask, Lady Tessa, for you to witness something for me. I've decided to claim the queen as my right."

Tess stopped so suddenly he walked into her. She stared at him with her mouth opened for several seconds. "If you want me to watch you actually claim the queen, then fuck no! You don't even…yuck! However, if you'd like me to be there when you declare her, then that's fine. It would be an honor."

"Good." That was all the warning she got. As soon as he uttered the word they were standing in the antechamber of the queen's personal suite. Mel was sitting in a large chair, apparently listening to her mother. Shamus bowed before them both.

"I think you might have taken a wrong—"

Shamus pulled Mel up from the chair with a hand behind her head. As she reached out and put her hand on his chest he growled deep and kissed her.

Tess felt the connection immediately. Her bond with them both was so powerful that she could feel the queen's need and Shamus' blood thicken in his veins. Need roared through Tess from them. Tess wanted to be anywhere but here. When they broke off the kiss he said the words to bond them.

"I claim you, Queen Melody, Mistress of Light, Keeper of Magic. I claim you as my mate, my life, my queen as my right of law. I am your king, your half, the shadow to your needs. I claim you, Melody. How say you?"

Tess standing there in cuff and shackle had just witnessed the most powerful union of all the worlds and burst out laughing at the queen's answer.

"What the fuck took you so long?"

~~~

Nathaniel felt the ground rumble beneath his feet. Something huge had shifted. When he reached for his gun he was both surprised and terrified at the same time that he came up empty handed. He looked around for cover just as the first change occurred.

The trees, lush before, now seemed to be greener. Their branches were fuller and they seemed to reach more toward the sky. Had he not thought he'd sound so stupid he would have said they seemed to be standing taller. Then the grounds all around him began to bloom. Deep colors of red and yellow erupted from the ground in the form of flowers. Fairies, colors as vast as the meadow began to appear. They seemed to be…to be kissing the flowers as they appeared. Birds began to sing. Nathaniel would swear that they had been doing so all along, but had only just noticed them. He knew, though, that it wasn't true. Something had happened, something huge and wonderful.

As he stood there watching the forest come alive, he felt someone come up behind him just seconds before he was aware. He turned quickly and was startled by a centaur.

"My lord," he said as he bowed before Nathaniel. And just like that, he knew who it was, his name. "I am to escort you to your residence, please?"

"Jacob? Your name is Jacob, isn't it? You're an ambassador to the queen. How do I know that?" He hadn't meant to sound panicky, but he heard it in his voice.
~~~

"It is your connection to the Lady Knight, my lord. She is part of this realm and has been for centuries. If you would follow me, I would see you to your residence."

Nathaniel took two steps then stopped. He looked around and then back at Jacob. Something had happened and he wasn't sure that all of it was as good as he had thought earlier.

"My lord?"

"Where's Tess? Lady Knight. Where is she right now? Something has…tell me where she is."

Jacob shifted on his hooves. He bowed his head low and didn't raise it again as he spoke. "Lady Knight, she has been taken, my lord. Her punishment will begin on the morrow. They have taken her to the dungeon in preparation."

"And where am I going? I know you said my residence, but where would that be?" Nathaniel knew when Jacob shifted again that he wasn't going to like the answer.

"I believe Lord Aaron will be able to answer your questions. It is to his residence that I am to take you. Lady Knight has requested that you be gone from Avalone tonight, sire. She wishes you to not witness the payment tomorrow."

Tess was so ready to toss him away. Nathaniel's heart ached suddenly. He realized that Jacob was still waiting. Then Nathaniel looked down at his arms. "They're fading. Why are the marks…it's happening, isn't it? The more she pulls away—no, the more I pull away from her, the more of her will disappear from me. Soon, she won't even be a memory, will she?" he said to Jacob.

"I do not know, my lord. No one has ever rejected the love of a fae before. But the queen assures me that once you step into the human world again another will be chosen for you. She would not have you go through your days without a mate."

For reasons he could not imagine that pissed Nathaniel off. What right did she have to choose another for him? What right…because he had given it to her. By rejecting Tess he had given the queen every right to whatever she wanted. Nathaniel looked to Jacob. “I want to go to Tess. Can you tell me how to get to her? Right now?”

“The dungeon, sire. Lady Knight resides in the castle dungeon until her lashing on the morrow at noon,” Jacob told him.

“Not if I have anything to say about it. Take me to see Shamus. Now, please.”

“The king? You wish an audience with the king?”

“Yes. With the king. I’m not sure what happened there, but I’m sure he’ll be more than willing to tell me.”

Chapter Twenty Two

Tess sat on the floor to her cell. The room wasn't all that bad, just slightly more damp than before when she'd been brought here long ago. The window was new, though the view left a lot to be desired. There were no bars on the wall, not even a door. Tess and prisoners like her were held with magic. Not that Tess had tried, but she knew that if she were to try and step through the opening, she would be bound within it with magic. At least until someone released her, and it would have to be the queen.

Looking at the purple stone on her food tray Tess wondered why she'd been sent a fairy stone. She preferred her solitude and knew whatever the fairy was supposed to tell her, she more than likely didn't want to hear. She turned to the window again.

When the voice began, Tess wasn't sure she was hearing it. Then after a minute, she realized she knew that voice. And the tone.

"Grandmother?"

As soon as Tess acknowledged her, her grandmother's image shimmered in the cell. It had been so long since Tess had seen her that her throat clogged tight with emotion.

"What the harrellish nipple do you think you're doing? Don't you think enough blood has been shed in this family? Think we need another martyr to give more? And sit up straight when I speak to you, young lady."

Tess straightened so quickly she bumped her head on the wall. She was nearly eleven thousand years old and her grandmother could make her feel ten again in no time.

"I broke the queen's law. It is the right—"

"Don't speak to me about rights. I know what they are. I helped write the damned things. And that's not what I asked you. Where is your mate? Why isn't he here with you in your hour of need?"

Tess bowed her head. She didn't want her grandmother to see the hurt and tears in her eyes. Tess thought she could take several beatings over the pain of her heart right now.

"He's gone back to the human race where he belongs. He doesn't want…he wants to remain vampire, not fae. Mel is to release him from our bond."

Tess could feel her grandmother trample through her mind. She didn't try and stop her. It would have hurt more and her grandmother would get what she wanted regardless.

"So he knows nothing of what he'd be. What he'd be able to do as a Fae." Tess didn't answer. "Tessa, does he know what happens to you without a mate, without him? More importantly, does he know that you love him?"

"Yes. He knows I love him. It didn't matter. He didn't want to know about fae. What does it matter anyway? He is what he wanted to be. Leave it go, Grandmother. I beg of you to let it go."

~~~
~~~

Neither said anything for some time. Tess was so lost in her heartache and misery that she didn't notice that she'd been put to sleep—the deep and magical sleep only a fae could survive. As soon as Tess was lifted and put to bed by her powerful grandmother, Tessa June, she picked up the purple stone and blew across it, bringing the small fairy to life.

When the heather fairy appeared in the deep purple hues of her kind Tessa June listened to Gardiana's message from Tessa May's mate, Nathaniel. Tessa June, for the first time in decades, the most powerful fae born second only to her granddaughter, smiled.

"Send for his Lordship Shamus. I wish an audience with him. And find Nathaniel. He may have already left this realm. I need to speak with him immediately."

"No, my lady, he has not. Master Knight Nathaniel seeks a meeting with our king as well. They meet—" Gardiana started.

"King," Tessa June exclaimed. "So he finally did it, did he? Good for him. Tell his Lordship the King that I wish an audience with him, hopefully with Nathaniel there as well. Tell the king that I will come to collect. Tell him that I will accept nothing but his complete cooperation. Tell him to meet me…"

"Shall I have him meet you at the Tree of Life, my lady? I know that others go there to see Lady Knight's release."

Tessa June looked at her only granddaughter. Her heart broke for her. The child had endured so much and now this.

"Yes. Tell him to meet me there. I've a few words to say to his lordship."

~~~

Tess woke to sunlight streaming through the window. At first she was confused, but suddenly she remembered where she was. Standing, she stretched long and hard and felt marginally better for it.
~~~

Tess wasn't worried about the lashes. She would heal. They would leave no scars and she would only have the memory of them too soon. No, that didn't bother her at all.

Looking down at her markings she was surprised that the band marking her as mated and bonded was still there. She would have thought that it would have faded by now. By her calculations Nathaniel had been gone from Avalone for more than twelve hours. More than enough time for them to begin their change of status. She traced her fingers over the small band that said both their names in her language and the date that they had mated.

Had Nathaniel stayed her mate the band would have widened over the years, filling in with the names of their children and their children's children. But by now, as had happened to her grandmother's, the band would turn black, become a single black band marking her as barren and unmated.

There was another tray, another stone, and another note. Every hour since she'd been brought in there had been the same thing, note and stone that came through the tray slot. And like all the other times, she ignored them both. Walking to the hanging sink Tess washed her face and then looked in the mirror.

Tess was fae, a warrior fae, and it showed in her features now as it had before. Her eyes, no longer human, looked back at her in the bright green color. There were dots of blues, yellows, and reds throughout. Her face was longer, thinner, and her lips full and lush. As she was the master, her elongated lobes at her ears sparkled and were studded with jewels—emeralds, rubies, and diamonds. Her crown, as a part of her heritage and the last of her kind born to a fae, sat upon her head for all to see.

But it was her wings that she had missed most of all. Spreading them wide, Tess marveled at their beauty. Open fully they each spanned four feet across, wide enough to carry her great distances. Their color was a deep blue with a plethora of other colors showing brightly throughout. Their radiant lighting brightened the room to an amazing brilliance.

"Lady Tess? You have a visitor. Lady Sara is here to see you. May I open the doorway, please?"

Tess looked at the person standing behind her, using the mirror in front of her to see. She was in the perfect position to see the entire room and her guard Kylard, who had stood outside since she'd been brought here. "Tell her to fuck off and to leave me alone. I no longer serve her. And I wish my peace."

"You have never learned any manners. I don't know why I thought now would be any different. Take down the door, Kylard. I'm going to have a talk with your stubborn mistress," Sara said as she stood to just the right of Tess's personal guard.

Tess ignored Sara once she had been let in the cell. Tess went about her business of getting dressed. She brushed her teeth and began to braid her hair. She would have had it cut, but that would have to wait now.

"If you don't speak to me I can't help you out of this mess you've gotten yourself into. And when I send a fairy to speak to you, I expect you to answer it. Come and sit down, Tess," Sara said.

"I'm not in a mess, Sara. And I've no wish to speak to you now or at any other time, thanks. Say whatever it is that's burning through you and leave. I have an…an event coming up and I—"

"Event? You call getting lashed two hundred times an event? What on earth would you call giving birth, I wonder."

Tess put the band in her hair just as the magic dropped from the door again. Her escort had just arrived and was standing outside waiting. She wasn't sure what they did it for, but she put her hands out to be cuffed. Tess hated Sara in that moment, hated her for what she reminded her of.

"Since that will never happen to me, I will call this whatever the fuck I want, an event. Goodbye, Sara. I want you to stay away from me."

"Tess, I'm so sorry. I never meant to—"

Tess turned her back. She didn't want anyone else to know her pain, and that was when she noticed Jacob. Damn it all to hell. "What are you doing here? I thought I gave you a direct order to stay away from these proceedings."

"Yes, my lady, you did. But the king overruled you. I'm to escort you to the field where the punishment will be given." Jacob looked—well, she would say he looked more confident. She would have to tell that to Shamus right after she kicked the shit out of him.

They were nearly to the open field when Tess stopped. The men at her back fell into her and the men to her sides and front were several steps ahead before they realized she had stopped. Once they surrounded her again, she looked at Kylard who looked very nervous. Before she could speak Shamus, or the new king, was in front of her.

"Lady Tessa. How are you feeling this fine day? Nice weather for a gathering, don't you think? The woodland fairies said they were to make it rain, but I asked them to wait until the night. I don't know, I thought it would put a dam—"

"What the fuck is going on here? Why are all these people here? I was told this would be private, only between me, the queen, and the handler."

Shamus nodded to the men and they stepped aside. When he touched her cuffs at her wrists they, along with the shackles at her ankles, dropped to the ground.

"Someone must have leaked it out. I wonder…oh well. No help for it now. Come along, my friend."

Tess didn't say another word. She was stunned at the amount of people there. She could even see that a pair of chairs had been set up near the tree, presumably for the king and queen themselves. Tess could see her grandmother talking with Sara as well. She dropped her head until Shamus had her standing next to the tree.

~~~

Nathaniel saw her the moment the men separated from around her. Her beauty took his breath away. The physical change alone was amazing, but it was more than that. It was her added confidence in herself.

Sara had already told him what had happened in the cell. He'd tried to tell her that Tess wouldn't go for it, but Sara said she had to try. Sara's other role in the plan for him was to distract Tess enough so that she wouldn't feel the magic shifting around her when beings showed up for her. And from the look on Tess's face, it had worked. She was surprised by them as much as he had been. He chuckled; they were here for Tess's event. Sara was pissed when Nathaniel laughed.

"It would serve you right if she used that whip on you. I've never seen a more suited couple than you two. I hope you know she only gets worse with age."

Nathaniel hoped so. He was looking forward to many years, many centuries, trying to make her happy. He started across the field to her.

Nathaniel had been very busy since Jacob had found him. He'd had a great deal to think about. The least of which was to take what he could have from her. He'd been an arrogant fool
~~~

and hoped that she would let him try again. He had spent a considerable amount of time with the new king too.

Shamus had claimed his own mate and had been equally claimed by her. It seemed as if neither of them cared what the shift from one being to the other had entailed, their love transcended through that. Shamus was now a true immortal.

"So long as Mellie is queen I will be at her side. And if need be, behind her or in front of her. And when she is ready, I will continue to be with her even in the Fade," Shamus had said with a sappy grin on his face.

"Fade? You mean death? Vampires do that. If something happens to their mates, they die as well."

"No. We will never die, Nathaniel. The Fade is just what it sounds like. We can fade from this realm into one of our own making. And if we are ever called upon again we can return. We are true immortals. So are you and Tess, well, until you actually leave her."

Nathaniel had been shocked by that. That and so many other things he'd been told and shown. James, Mel's father, brought him a large book, much like the one he'd been shown before when he'd been trying to figure out what she was. The book contained their triumphs and the lineage he now descended from. Well, he thought, he would be a descended from as soon as he accepted everything from Tess, He just hoped he hadn't screwed it up too much and she told him to fuck off—which she probably would anyway. Aaron met him about halfway across the field.

"You ready for this? You know she's going to be more than pissed about this? And she'll flay you alive for interfering."

Nathaniel grinned. "Yeah, but the make up sex will be great."

They continued on several more feet before Nathaniel spoke again. “I love her. I love her more than I ever thought possible. And the thought of her being whipped…” He was unable to continue that thought.

“She won’t. What you’ve done is brilliant. If you pull this off, I’m telling everyone this was my idea. If it’s a failure, then it’s all you.”

Before Nathaniel could answer, they were standing before Tess. Christ, but she was pissed.

Anger boiled off her. Her wings, tight against her back, quivered. Nathaniel could feel his own begin to do the same. His need to cover her in them and protect her was profound.

“Tess, you look lovely to—”

“Fuck off! What the hell are you doing here? You were to be taken back to him.” Tess nearly impaled Aaron with her finger when she pointed at him. “And what the hell are you…no, you didn’t. You idiot! You didn’t accept him back, did you?”

Aaron only grinned in answer.

Nathaniel had been told that he needed to be accepted back as a vampire and human so that Mel could complete his moving back among the humans. The issue had never come up because Nathaniel had never answered the queen’s summons to be changed. Aaron had never been asked because Nathaniel had decided not to change. He would tell her later, much later.

Before anything else could be said Mel called the punishment to order. Tess was led to the tree, to be brought before the queen to have her crime read to the masses then sentencing carried out.

“Tessa May Knight, warrior fae, Master At Arms, Brianal Guard, you are brought here to be punished for the act of treason against the queen. How do you plead?”

Nathaniel stood. “My queen, I am mate to the Lady Knight, master as her equal. I am…I am…shit! I am warrior fae, Master at Arms, Brianal Guard. I wish to speak on behalf of my men.”

Mel sat back down as she spoke with a huge smile on her face. “Go ahead, Master Knight, but you may want to practice your title a bit more. I’m pretty sure ‘shit’ isn’t a part of it.”

Nathaniel flushed. “Yes, my lady. I am mate to the Lady Knight and as such, willingly take her first lash.”

“You idiot! You can’t do…Queen, you can’t let him do that. This is…he was supposed to be gone. That’s what he wanted.”

“Well, I think he’s changed his mind. Though I can’t understand why he’d want to stay with one such as you, he seems to want to be with you. I grant your request, Master Knight. Proceed.”

“Hold, my queen.” The room seemed to turn as one as the man now standing made his way to the couple. “I am Master Vampire Aaron Xavier MacManus and as my right as one who owes Lady Knight the life of my unborn child, I willingly take her second lash.”

“Thank you, Master MacManus, your request is also granted. Is there anyone else who feels inclined to take a lash for Lady Knight?” Mel asked the people there waiting.

As a whole, the field of people stood—seven thousand beings—to take one for Tess, their love and respect for the fae evident in their faces.

“I see. Please be seated everyone.” Nathaniel held his breath as Mel came across the short distance with Shamus at her side. “You have a great deal of loyalty it seems.”

“I didn’t ask them to do this. They shouldn’t even be here. You know that as well as I do,” Tess whispered.

"No, you did not. They gave it to you willingly. That is what makes it all the more special, don't you think, Lady Tess? I accept the request of all these beings to take your—"

"Don't do that. This is about—" Tess started, only to be stopped by the queen's hand.

"You'd do well to behave and not interrupt me again, Tessa. As I was saying, I accept the request of all these present to take your lash. I have more than lashes you are required to receive. You will choose who takes them for you."

Nathaniel stood behind Tess, wrapped his arms around her waist, and brought her body to his. He could feel her pain and thought it was his own. And her pride at the people here today and what they had given her. He pulled her tighter still.

"Please don't do this. I'll do anything else. I beg of you." No one save the people in their small circle could hear Tess's whispered request.

Shamus cleared his throat and continued. "You choose who takes them, Tess, or give Nathaniel his part of you. Take him as your mate and we'll go home and celebrate."

"You will blackmail me, Shamus? Me? You know that I—"

"It isn't blackmail if everyone is willing. I assure you it will be no hardship on him. He knows what you give him and what he gives you. He wants this, wants it as badly as you."

Nathaniel turned her in his arms. "Let me try to say this part without screwing this up. I practiced this one more."

"Don't do this, Nathaniel. It's not necessary," Tess said as he dropped to the ground before her.

"Hush. You'll mess me up. Let me see…oh yeah. Tessa May Knight, Master Warrior Fae, my mate, my love. I accept all that you are, all that you have, and all that you give to me. I accept your heritage as my own, your lineage, your everything in my keeping. I willingly take unto me all that you have been and will be. I willingly become your half, your equal, your mate. As your mate, I become fae, your fae, your mate, your love."

Tess was crying as he finished and he reached up with his thumb and brushed away her tears. "Are you sure? There is no turning back if I answer you," she whispered.

"Love, I have never been surer of anything in my entire life."

"Then I accept you." He was surprised by the simplicity of her answer and was startled when those next to them took a step away. Suddenly, magic that she poured into him hit him hard. His last conscious thought was, mother fuck!

Chapter Twenty Three

Tess was just waking up when she felt Nathaniel beside her stir. It had been less than two hours since they'd left the field and she had been scared to death. When his hand ran from her thigh to her ass Tess felt the first stirrings of desire start to rise.

"I want you, Tess. My cock is hard and aching to be deep inside of you. Please tell me no one can feel us while we're in here."

Tess rolled over to face him and reached up to trace the markings on his face. Then the one over his heart. "We are in one of the rooms at the castle. No one will feel our need unless we open the door. The queen gave us this part of the castle for that reason."

Nathaniel's mumbled, "Thank you, Mel" was lost against Tess's mouth.

Tess felt his heat and need hard and fast. Her body, already primed to take his, gushed with cream as soon as he touched her. Now it was sharp. With his mouth moving down her body to her breast it was everything she could do not to scream when he took her nipple into his mouth, even as he slid his fingers deep into her.

When his mouth moved to her belly his tongue swirled in her navel. The sensation was amazing and she could feel it race more hot blood to her already overheated pussy.

"Please, Nathaniel. I need you. My body is on fire for yours. Please? We can take our time the next time. Not now."

"I don't know if there will ever be a time when I don't need you quick. Christ, the way you smell makes me hurt to be inside of you." He nibbled again before he shifted. "Roll over. I want to pound your sweet pussy from behind and fuck you until you scream."

Tess rolled over when Nathaniel moved to his knees. When she was on her own knees and her ass high, legs apart, he entered her with his fingers.

"Hot and wet. I want to lick you, but I know that if I start tasting you I won't want to quit. I need to feel you tighten around me, milk my cock hard when you come."

"Please, Nathaniel. I need you now. Fuck me, please?"

Before she could finish begging he slammed deep into her. Her scream ripped from her throat as she came. Her climax tore through her so quickly she had no time to appreciate his holding back while she came.

"Again. I need to come again. Please come with me, fill me with your cum."

As he pulled out to near the tip of his cock he leaned forward and bit her shoulder. Another climax, quick and hard, punched through her. When Nathaniel reached around and pulled on her clit as he rocked hard into her she felt another one building.

"You're fertile, Tess. I can feel it in you. Your body is telling me it's ready to receive me. When we come, this time together, I'm going to fill you with my seed. I want to fill your belly with our child. Will you accept, Tess? Will you let me give you our child?"

When he rocked into her again she knew that she wanted his child, their child. So when he pulled to the tip again she told him so. "Fill me, Master Knight. Give me your seed."

His cock slammed into her again and again. Each time he touched her deep, touched her womb. With his roar of release, she went with him. Her body pulled and tightened around his with each jerk of his cock.

Finally, when she could no longer stay upright on her knees, she collapsed, bringing him with her. Even as she drifted to sleep sated and relaxed she thought of the babe they had just created and smiled. She was no longer the last of her kind.

~~~

Nathaniel woke in the empty bed. He was a little disappointed at first until he reached out to find her. She was with her men, running them through their drills.

"You should have stayed here. I had plans for your delicious body. First I was going to wake you with my face buried between your legs. I meant to drink from you until you filled me as I filled you. Then I…Tess? Fuck, your men… they know that I need you because you're not here."

He felt her laughter first. "Yes. They can feel what you do to me. And if there are several hundred babies born nine months from this day I will not be surprised. I'm coming home, but you need to get your lazy ass out of bed from now on. I couldn't wake you."

"That's because you wore me out. Come home now and I'll make it worth your while."

"We have a meeting with the queen. You come here. You've totally ruined my men for any more work today so we
~~~

might as well get this over with. You can shift or fly and I'll be waiting."

Nathaniel was there in ten minutes. He might have been sooner, but he was still getting used to the wings thing. He smiled down at her when she reached up and pulled grass from his hair.

"The ground jumped up and hit me when I was flying along minding my own business. I tried to fight it off, but there was no stopping it."

"Sure there was. I think you should practice getting around more for now. Draco said he'd help you. And your sword is finished."

They went to the blacksmith first. The man had been so honored to make his sword that he'd had to ask Tess about it later. He was humbled by her response.

"There are only five people in the realm that can make swords. The Wallace family, the man who did this for you, have been making them for centuries. Sherman, Mel's pervious mate, had had his sons put into the prison for what Sherman deemed their fault. The sword had not wanted him to own it."

"Excuse me? The sword didn't want Sherman to own it?" He looked at the small smithy where he had gotten his sword made. "Magic. It's all about magic here. I'll have to get used to that. So he had the sons put into the dungeon. Then what?"

"Then Wallace could no longer make swords for the realm. You asking him to make yours was a great honor to him and his family. He will no longer be made to feel the failure. You have restored his faith in himself."

By the time they reached the castle Nathaniel was feeling very good. He had a life vastly different than the one before, and his mate. Smiling, he thought he could get used to this.

When they entered the personal chambers of the king and queen Nathaniel was whistling.

"This is just a formality. I want to offer you both the job of commanding my fae. Once you accept, you will both have a mark, a sigil that signifies you as such. Do you accept?

They had talked about it and both agreed they would. The sigil, the mark of the king and queen of Molavonta and Avalone combined, would be branded into their skin forevermore. Nodding their acceptance, both Mel and Shamus stepped forward and touched them with the ceremonial dagger. The brand was painless and beautiful.

The sigil would be on each of their children until they reached the age of maturity and would be able to decide then if this was the path they wished to take. Then the mark would be either removed or left in place depending on the answer.

The crossed claymores were in vivid detail and full of color. The Tree of Life, just behind the swords, was the mark of the queen. It too was alive with color. And anyone who saw the mark would know that they were under the protection of the queen and king. Harm against them or their family meant certain death.

Tess and Nathaniel left the castle to begin their lives as mates, never to leave the realm again without the expressed permission of the monarchs. Life had a way of making such rules obsolete.

About the Author

I woke up one morning and decided to give play time to the people in my head who were keeping me awake. Little did I know that they would be so relentless and want their time right now! I wrote for the pure joy of it and to entertain my family and friends. But mostly it was to get more than an hour of sleep without a story playing out. Of course, the more I write, the more they want. So…well, as a result of sleepless days (I work through the night as a gun toting grandma – nope not a vigilantly but an armed security guard) I have lots of stories written.

Hello! My name is Kathi Barton and I'm an author. I have been married to my very best friend Sonny for at times seems several lifetimes – in a good way, honey. And together we have three wonderful children and then the ones we brought into the world - Paul and Dale Barton, Jason and Wendy Barton and Danielle and Ben Conklin. They have given us seven of the greatest treasures on Earth. They don't live at home seven days a week! No, seriously, seven grandchildren – Gavin, Spring, Ben, Trinity, Sarah, Kelly and Kian.

www.ingramcontent.com/pod-product-compliance
Lightning Source LLC
Chambersburg PA
CBHW020610180626
46810CB00007B/2720

* 9 7 8 1 9 3 8 9 6 1 1 1 3 *